Advance Praise for *BOCK'S CANYON*

Popular western author Dan Baldwin put his boots on the ground where his character Brodie Dephrane literally walked in Arizona and New Mexico, on his way to Bock's Canyon. Baldwin paints the west with precise strokes, inviting the reader to take another step with him. In this quick paced western thriller, young Brodie had no choice but to watch the abuse and murder of his mother by a gang of killers. Shot and left for dead by Tule Henderson, Brodie survives and resolves to render justice. The novel follows Brodie through the years as he grows up and, taking advantage of a colorful band of acquaintances, becomes adept at tracking and calculating in revenge. Brodie's quest is a gritty quixotic journey. Brodie leaves his Dulcinea, Enid McCutchen, to complete his grisly resolve then return. Accompanying Brodie much of the way is the cajun Montreur, whose spice is not just for cuisine but his focused outlook. The wily and dangerous Tule knows he's being hunted and litters the towns and mines with spies and traps. Riding alongside Brodie, the reader must keep a practiced eye on the landscape. *"Bock's Canyon"* is a winner.

~George Sewell Author: *The Krismer* and *Ashes, Urns and What Did You Say?*

Comments on Dan Baldwin's *CALDERA* SERIES

Dan Baldwin's *CALDERA* is, first and foremost, a fast-paced, fun read. In HORIZON'S WEST, Jim Kitses seminal study of the classic Western, the founding of the West was essentially a dust-up between civilization (order) and wilderness (chaos). Dan paints that picture with a brush of fine details. The characters are bigger than life and the reader gets a sense of the tough skinned, tough minded men and women who settled what would eventually become the state of Arizona. But the story isn't just a typical rendition of the White American settlers (order) triumphant over the landscape and the savages (chaos) who live there. The settlers bring a great deal of their own chaos and the native Pimas have an established civilization suitable for its surroundings. The read is a wonderful blend of fact and fiction, well researched and well told. I highly recommend this book to anyone interested in the Old West, powerful characters or just great story telling.

~Micah S. Hackler, Author, Sheriff Lansing Mysteries

As a writer, I'm always pleased to see another writer succeed. As a professional freelance editor, I'm even more pleased when an editing client succeeds. I read a lot of manuscripts. Every now and then, one comes along that screams for a sequel. That was the case with *Caldera*. Although *Caldera* is a long novel that left me more than satisfied, it was such an excellent story that it also left me hungering for more. When Dan told me he was going to write Man on Fire, a sequel to *Caldera*, I didn't really care whether I got to edit it. I just wanted to read it. And not to let the cat out of the bag, but I have it on good authority that Dan is planning at least two more books in the *Caldera* series. I predict this will be a saga in the grand style of James A. Michener, but without all the misplaced modifiers.

~Harvey Stanbrough, poet, essayist, fictionist, editor, instructor and Pulitzer Prize nominee for poetry. Author *Writing Realistic Dialog & Flash Fiction; Punctuation for Writers; Six Days in May; Beyond the Masks; Always in Your Face.*

BOCK'S CANYON

DAN BALDWIN

Bock's Canyon
A Four Knights Press publication
Copyright © 2015 by Dan Baldwin
Printed in the United States of America
All rights reserved.
* * * * *

* * * * *

Disclaimer
This is a work of fiction, a product of the author's imagination. Any resemblance or similarity to any actual events or persons, living or dead, is purely coincidental.

* * * * *

Credits
Cover photo by Dan Baldwin
Formatting by Debora Lewis arenapublishing.org

ISBN-13: 978-1519695888
ISBN-10: 1519695888

Acknowledgements

Mary Baldwin for editing and patience
above and beyond the call of duty.

Debora K. Lewis, ArenaPublishing.org,
for her usual excellence in formatting and cover design.

BOCK'S CANYON

Part One: Brodie

1

"You goin' up against a .44 with just a pen knife, kid?"

"It's all I got."

"It ain't enough."

The kid screamed and rushed the big man. His small knife cut into the man's heavy coat, but never struck muscle or even flesh. A second later he was sprawled across his father's body on the packed dirt floor of their small cabin. Jocko Henderson looked down on the pitiful sight. "You got more sand than your daddy, boy. Don't let it get you killed."

"Leave my mama alone!"

Tule Henderson, a shorter and more compact version of his brother, turned his attention from the woman. "Kill that little bastard. He's crampin' my style."

"Shut up, Tule."

The woman pleaded. "Don't hurt my boy. Please don't…."

Tule slapped her across the face. He ripped the top of her dress and threw her across the room onto a bed made of rough-cut wood. "Me first, Jocko."

"Take your time." Jocko pulled a twist of tobacco and took a bite.

Tule crossed the room, watching with a smile as the woman crawled back on the worn blankets. "I'm carrying a child. Please…."

"You're going to be carrying a lot more 'n that, lady."

Tule dropped his suspenders, threw his stained felt hat to the floor and crawled on the bed. "Let's see what you got to show me." He grabbed her dress with a laugh.

The boy jumped up, his hands red with his father's blood, but Jocko easily grabbed him by the neck and threw him against the wall. "I ought to kill you right now, boy."

The kid steadied himself against the wall. "You better."

Jocko laughed.

The woman screamed.

The kid made another rush, his screams drowning those of his mother. Jocko caught him by the throat again, dragged him across the room and shoved him against the small woodstove in the corner of the one-room cabin. The iron was still hot from the morning's meal, but the pain of seeing what Tule was doing to his mother drove away the pain of the hot metal.

"Don't hurt her no more!"

"Woman was born to hurt, boy. Don't you know that?" Jocko held the boy to the stove with one hand and scratched his privates with the other. "Now, you watch and learn."

Tule had mounted the woman, holding his hand over her mouth to shut out her screams. The kid looked away. Jocko moved quickly and held the boy's head between his hands, forcing him to watch. "Look!"

When Tule finished, Jocko took his turn and Jocko was a rough man. Tule, like his brother, held the boy's head so that he was forced to watch.

Tule shoved a torn rag in the kid's mouth to stop his shouting. He sat down on a bench against the wall and watched his brother at work.

The kid struggled and wept.

When Jocko finished, he stood up and buttoned his britches. He looked down at the woman and grunted. He strapped on his belt. "Let's go."

Tule stood up. "I want me one more time."

"No, you don't."

"And why not big brother?"

"She's dead."

The kid, no longer screaming, no longer weeping, just stared at Jocko.

"You better kill that boy while you can, big brother."

2

Jocko laughed. "I like him. But, you're right." He stepped to the front door and shouted to someone outside. "Henry! Get in here."

A small man smelling of whiskey rushed in. "My turn?"

"You missed out on your turn."

"The hell I did."

Tule laughed. "Sure thing, Henry, if you don't mind 'em a little stiff."

"What the hell."

Tule said, "Better hurry. She's turning cold on you."

Jocko grabbed Henry by his shirt and shoved him toward the boy. "I got something better for you. Kill 'im."

Henry looked to the woman and then to the kid. He smiled and pulled out his long knife.

Tule said, "We ain't got time for amusements."

"Get it over with," Jocko said.

Henry grabbed the boy and jerked him across the room. The kid rolled toward the door and ran outside. Henry grabbed his pistol and followed.

The boy was no more than ten yards from the house when Henry shot him in the back. He fell into the dirt and dust, rolled over once and didn't move.

"Let's git," Tule said.

The three men mounted up and rode away.

Three days later two riders coming out of Goodridge followed the San Juan, a muddy and meandering waterway through the rust red buttes and mesas of southern Utah. Each man grinned when they saw the feature locals called "Mexican Hat." The pinnacle was topped by what appeared to be an upturned sombrero. The hat could be seen for miles and it marked the small ranch of Marsh and Callie Duphrane, a single room cabin on a ledge above the cottonwoods and reeds that lined the river.

Dukie Hedgeway halted and wiped the sweat from his forehead. "It's about dinner time, don't you think?"

Juan Galleta nodded. "It is always dinner time at Senora Duphrane's home."

"Good folks." He kicked his spurs gently against the sides of his horse. Juan followed. Both men slowed and came to a halt when the wind shifted and the smell of old death assaulted their senses.

"This is not good," Galleta said.

"Too much for a dead pole cat. C'mon!"

The men rode swiftly to the cabin and covered their lower faces with their bandanas as they dismounted. Inside they recoiled at the sight. The bodies of Marsh and Callie Duphrane were bloated to point of bursting. The men gagged. Marsh's head had been blown half off. Juan grabbed a blanket hanging over a window and covered Callie's body. Dukie walked to the door and looked out. Someone was in the shadows beneath a cottonwood. "Damnation, Juan, it's Brodie's. He ain't all swole up either. Brodie's."

The men rushed to the cottonwood and turned over the boy."

"He's been shot in the heart," Dukie said.

"We must get him to town, Dukie. The doctor...."

"Moving might kill him. He's awful poorly."

"Then we had best move quickly."

Juan pulled the front door off its leather hinges and they constructed a crude stretcher pulled by his horse. They covered Brodie with a blanket and tied him to the stretcher.

"Take it easy going up the hill. Once we get to the road the trip will be easier on him," Dukie said.

"What about... you, know... the animals will get in there."

"We'll come back later and do what we can for 'em. Right now we got this kid to worry about."

Juan nodded toward the cabin. "Navajo?"

"Hell, there ain't been no Navajo around here since Kit Carson."

"You know better."

"Renegade Navajos didn't do this, Juan."

"You sure?"

"Tobacco spit. It's on the kid's face mixed in with all that blood. And Miss Callie, it's on her face. White men did this."

"White men soon to die, my friend. Soon to die."

"That's for later." Dukie looked over to the kid on the stretcher. "Damnation. Ten years old is a hell of a time to have to grow up."

"Let us ride easy and see that he does."

2

Hedgeway stuck his head into the doorway of Frenchy McCutchen's barbershop. "How's the kid?"

McCutchen stopped sweeping and sat down. He indicated with a head movement for Hedgeway to do the same. "He gonna make it, doc?"

"Damn it, I ain't no doc."

"You're the closest thing we got, Frenchy. The kid?"

"He's a tough little son of a bitch. I think he'll pull through."

"It's an amazement."

"Another half inch… hell, a hair closer to his heart and we'd have buried him out there with his folks."

McCutchen spun the broom in his hand, swirling up bits of hair and dust. "Any idea of who did it?"

"Nah. Brodie's the only one who knows. Is he still out?"

"Yeah. I'll give you a shout when he comes around. You got to do something about this."

"Me?"

"You found 'em, you and Juan. That makes it your responsibility."

"That's something for the law, Frenchy."

"You're the closest thing we got." McCutchen grinned.

"Damn you."

Brodie Duphrane struggled his way to awareness a day later. McCutchen got him to drink some water and later fed him some broth. The kid nodded thanks and fell asleep. When he awoke some hours later, Hedgeway and Galleta were talking to McCutchen in the front of the barber shop.

"Mr. Hedgeway?"

The three men turned and stepped into the back room. Hedgeway sat on the edge of the bed as the others stood by.

"How are you doing, Brodie?"

"Those men, they killed my momma."

Hedgeway nodded for the two men to leave. They took the hint and left the room, but Galleta stood just outside the open door, listening.

"I hate to do this so soon, Brodie, but I have to talk to you some about what happened. Are you up to it?"

"Yes, sir. My folks?" Brodie coughed and winced from the pain.

"We buried 'em together out there under Mexican Hat. We carved their names on a rock and everything.

"About what happened...."

"Will you take me out there, Mr. Hedgeway? I got to put some flowers on momma's grave."

"Sure, Brodie. Your dad, too."

"No."

"Why not?"

"I'm going to piss on it." He coughed, worse than before, and turned pale.

Hedgeway shouted, "Frenchy!"

McCutchen rushed in and squatted down by the bed. Brodie continued coughing. "You boys better git. I got my hands full here." He turned his full attention to the kid.

Hedgeway and Galleta left and crossed the street to the Tolable Saloon, the fanciest business in Goodridge. It was a narrow building with a bar running two thirds of the way down opening to a gambling area with two tables in the rear. The bar was made of polished wood, brass fittings and a large mirror and had been hauled in from Prescott down in Arizona. Two men played a lazy game of poker. They nodded a hello as the Hedgeway and Galleta stepped up to the bar.

The owner and bartender, Jack Tolable, served two mugs of beer. "How's Brodie?"

"He's going to make it," Hedgeway said.

"Any idea who... you know?"

"He's too weak to talk. We'll find out in a day or so I think."

"When you do…" Tolable pulled out a sawed off shotgun from beneath the counter. "Don't leave me out of it."

Galleta took several swallows of the warm beer. "I hate to say this, my friends, but whoever did this is no longer in this part of the country."

"We'll see."

"There is hope. And then there is what is."

"Like I said, we'll see."

"Snakes. They strike and then run for cover."

Tolable placed the shotgun beneath the counter. "Damn. I was hoping to use this on those sons of bitches."

Galleta swallowed more beer and placed the mug on the bar. "Perhaps."

Hedgeway looked out the door to the barbershop. "It all depends on Brodie."

Hedgeway and Galleta owned a small ranch several miles upriver from Goodridge, not too far from the Duphrane place. They took time away from their chores to clean up the blood and destruction at the cabin and to build and hang a new door.

"Brodie can't run this place by himself, Dukie."

"No. But I've been thinking about that."

"What have you been thinking and I believe I like it already."

"Yeah. We could buy this place from him; he's the legal owner now."

"The money would take care of his needs for some time."

"It's an idea."

"And a good one. But first…."

"Yeah. Let's get back into town."

Brodie was sitting up in bed. His color had returned and his cough was persistent, but controllable. Hedgeway sat down on a stool by the bed. "I have to talk to you about what happened, Brodie. Can you handle that now?"

"Yes, sir."

"Who did this?"

"There was two of 'em, Mr. Hedgeway. They just showed up at the door. They were looking for trouble. I could tell right away even if my old man…." Brodie looked away.

"Tell me about it, Brodie. I got to know."

"That bastard just let 'em in." Brodie took in a long breath. "You should have tossed him into the river, Mr. Hedgeway. He don't deserve to be with momma."

"Damn, Brodie."

"He died on his knees. Take the woman, he said, just don't kill me. The big man, he laughed and shot half my old man's head off." Brodie coughed and caught his breath. "Then they—"

"Yeah. Did you recognize these men?"

"No, sir. I never seen 'em before."

"What did they look like? Did you catch their names?"

"Jacko. Jacko was the big one. Tule, the other, he was a lot like the other, only smaller."

"Go on."

Brodie described the killers in detail and even remembered details about their horses. "You're going after them aren't you?"

"As best we can. Juan and I tracked 'em after we brought you into town. We lost their trail out in the mesas south of your place. Now that we got something to work with—"

"They're long gone, ain't they?"

Hedgeway sighed. "Yeah."

"I figured."

"We'll get the word out. Here and down into Arizona, too. These men are going to pay for what they did, son. If we don't get 'em, somebody else will. I promise you that."

"What's going to happen to me?"

"Well, son, I have a few ideas about that."

3

Jacko and Tule Henderson were never caught. Word occasionally came in about men fitting their description and when the sightings were within a reasonable distance, Hedgeway and Galleta and sometimes a few other men from town rode out to track them down. The leads always proved to be false or too late for vengeance. The two ranchers raised Brodie as if he was a little brother and by the age of sixteen he was practically a full-grown man. The people of Goodridge became surrogate aunts and uncles, a responsibility made easier by the boy's easy-going and friendly nature.

He worked hard on the expanded D and J Ranch and proved himself to be a good and responsible hand. His adoptive brothers saw to it that he was also a well-rounded man. Goodridge didn't have a formal school, but it did have a few well-educated women who had books, patience, a bit of spare time and a need for extra cash. Several days a week Brodie left his chores on the ranch and rode into town for his lessons. He learned reading, writing, and math and even developed a taste for literature.

When Brodie complained in the early years about having to study, Hedgeway put matters into perspective. "This land's going to be won by force, by men tough enough to tame it. But it's going to be run by the thinkers – lawyers and bankers and such. If we're going to hold on to what we've built here, we have to be smarter than they are."

"Yes, sir."

"Me and Juan, we won this ranch. It's going to be up to you to keep it."

During those years Brodie also became one of the best shots with pistol and rifle in southern Utah. He invested a significant portion of his salary in ammunition and a large part of his limited free time in shooting practice. He was never shy about the reason for all the practice. Hedgeway interrupted his practice one day.

"Good shooting, Brodie."

"Thanks."

"You've been shooting off your mouth, too. Not so good."

Brodie dumped the shells from his revolver, adding to the substantial pile near his feet. He reloaded. "What do you mean?"

"You practice for Tule Henderson."

"Everybody knows that."

"And that is the problem. You talk too much."

"I don't understand."

"Do you think you will cross paths with Henderson? After all these years?"

"It's what I want to happen."

Hedgeway sighed. "When you hunt mountain lion, do you stand up and shout? 'Hey, mister mountain lion, here I am.'"

"Of course not."

"Hunting a man is far more dangerous. Juan says when words leave somebody's mouth they fly to where they can do the most harm."

"You think Henderson knows I'll be coming for him some day?"

"I think you should stop shouting."

"Shoot, don't shout. I get it."

Hedgeway spent the next couple of hours practicing with the younger man. Brodie never spoke of Tule Henderson again.

He made regular visits to his old home and planted desert flowers on and around his mother's grave. On his first trip to the site he had kicked over the wooden cross on his father's grave and, true to his word, pissed on the mound of red earth covering the man.

Later that long ago day Galleta took him for a walk near the ranch house. "What has happened to you is painful, I know. But you must learn from it as a man does."

"I learned plenty."

"And that is what concerns me. We move through life in the pathways we have been shown. Your father showed you a poor and twisted way through the world. A man can always find a better path if he is prepared to seek it."

"What are you getting at Mr. Galleta?"

"Your father was not much of a man."

"He wasn't a man at all."

"That is one of the paths I speak of."

"Don't you worry, Mr. Galleta. I ain't going to turn out like him."

"I respected your mother. She was a good woman."

"She was…." Brodie looked away.

"A woman deserves respect, Brodie. She may be a good woman, like your mother, she may be a saint or a whore in some crib, but she deserves respect. Promise me you'll show them that respect – always and to all women."

"I promise."

"There is one more thing. Your mother was a strong woman in many ways, but she needed the strength of a man to survive."

"She didn't have none of that. She was sickly mostly."

"We must be that strength, Brodie. We must respect, but we must also always protect them. They are the real future of this land."

"I… yes, sir."

"Your word?"

"Given."

The two shook hands. Galleta patted Brodie on the back as they walked back to the ranch house. "And one thing, Brodie. This talk, let us not speak of it to Dukie."

"That's all right, Mr. Galleta."

"Why do you say that?"

"We had the same talk last week."

Brodie took the lessons to heart. The only trouble he ever had in town occurred when he was fifteen. Late in the day riding home after one of his classes he saw two young men teasing Frenchy McCutchen's daughter, Enid. The boys, a year or two older than Brodie, were out of line, but they meant no real harm. Brodie rode up quickly and jumped from his horse onto the larger of the two young men. He was beaten in the fight that followed, but the older boys' aching muscles, cuts and bruises the next day left them with no feeling of victory.

One of the shop owners whisked Enid into her shop as the fighting began. They watched and when it ended the owner refused to let her run out to thank the young man who had fought for her. When Brodie mounted his horse and rode away he heard a tapping on the shop window. Enid smiled and waved from inside. He tipped his hat and rode off. A week later while attending one of his classes he opened one of the books his instructor kept for him. Inside was a cut-paper heart with a pencil drawing of a flower and the name Enid.

Brodie's chores often took him by the cabin where he had been raised. He never went in to collect any belongings or memorabilia and chose always to ride on by. One Sunday after his regular target practice down on the banks of the San Juan he rode over to the place. He stared at the run down structure for some time. Finally he dismounted and collected wood and brush, which he piled into the old cabin. He set it on fire, mounted up and rode off a short distance to watch the flames consume the building.

Hedgeway and Galleta noticed the smoke and quickly rode toward the source. When they reached the ridge overlooking the cabin they halted and watched for a moment. Hedgeway nodded back toward the ranch and the men rode away. Brodie never saw them. When the cabin was nothing more than ashes he returned to the ranch. No one ever mentioned the incident.

Brodie's seventeenth birthday turned out to be quite an event, not only for the young man, but for the citizens of Goodridge. Hedgeway and Galleta arranged for a surprise party in town – the townsfolk happy to arrange a break in their routine. The party was held in the back of Tolable's Saloon, which proved to be a delight to the town's womenfolk who had never seen the inside except in quick and hidden glances through the door as they walked by. Several of them giggled now and then as if getting away with some mild, secret sin.

Enid McCutchen brought a birthday cake she had baked and decorated. Hedgeway and Galleta paid for beer, whiskey and champagne for the one-hour duration of the party. Hedgeway and McCutchen pulled Brodie to the bar.

"Well, boy, this is it," McCutchen said.

"What is 'it'?"

Tolable set up three glasses of beer and three shots of whiskey. "*This* is it.'"

Galleta rushed in. "Amigos! You are leaving me out of the ceremony?"

Tolable poured another beer and another shot.

Galleta raised his glass. "Salud y pesatas."

"Health and wealth," Hedgeway said.

The three men killed their whiskey quickly and looked to Brodie. The young man took a sip and blinked quickly. "Whoa!"

"Kill it," McCutchen said.

Brodie swallowed the shot and fought off a cough.

The older men laughed. Hedgeway shoved the beer forward. "Now you know why they call this a chaser."

Brodie took the beer.

McCutchen said, "Speaking of chasers…." He pointed toward Enid who stood by the birthday cake. "Young Adleson's been making eyes at my daughter all afternoon. He'll be making his move pretty soon."

"Excuse me," Brodie said. He quickly made his way across the room to Enid.

Galleta said, "I wonder who is chasing who."

Hedgeway said, "I think she's getting ready to hogtie somebody with a matrimonial rope, I do."

McCutchen said, "I can't think of a better man. Gentlemen a toast – to what may be."

After the toast Hedgeway spoke in a more serious tone. "Speaking of what may be, it's time don't you think, Juan?"

"Si."

Hedgeway slapped his hand on the bar several times. "People! People! People! I got something to say!" The room noise became silence as everyone looked to the bar. Hedgeway stood on the foot rail to give himself a bit of extra height. "Me and Juan got something to say."

He paused. Hedgeway cleared his throat. "A few years back we found this birthday boy…." The people around Brodie shouted their approval. Hedgeway motioned for silence. "Despite certain distractions…." He pointed toward Enid, who blushed. "… the boy turned out to be a good man, a good hand and…a good son." Galleta noticed a slight tearing up in his partner's eyes.

It became Brodie's turn to blush. He blinked several times and Enid unconsciously took his hand.

"Well, said, my friend," Galleta said.

Hedgeway cleared his throat again. "So me and Juan a while back decided it was high time to turn this hand into a partner." He looked over to Tolable. "Jack, if you will, sir."

Tolable reached under the bar and brought out a large wooden sign painted white with bold black lettering – HGD Ranch. The crowd of friends and neighbors cheered. Brodie, in a mild daze, moved to the bar and looked at the sign.

"You sure," he said.

Hedgeway said, "We've been talkin' about it long enough. It's a time for getting on with things the way they ought to be."

Galleta pounded Brodie's shoulder. "We shall give it a try for the next twenty or thirty years. If that works out, we shall make it permanent."

They laughed, shook hands and then hugged each other.

Tolable said, "Well, this is surely the most momentous event in our young friend's life, eh?"

"Maybe," Hedgeway said.

"What do you mean, for Chrissakes?"

"It all depends."

"Depends on what?"

Galleta laughed and slapped Brodie. "On whether he kisses the girl or not." He shoved Brodie into the crowd toward Enid.

The four men completed another round of drinks when they noticed an old man standing in the door of the saloon. He was waving and trying to get their attention.

"Who is that?" McCutchen asked.

Tolable shook his head. "Don't know him."

Hedgeway said, "It's Si Vaughn."

"Like I said, who is that?"

"He used to be what they call a Mountain Man in the old days. He mostly keeps to himself, traps some, does a bit of trading." Hedgeway waved the old man in, but Vaughn shook his head and motioned for him to come out. "I'll see what the old coot wants." He left the party. Outside, Vaughn pulled him from the door.

"I didn't want to break up the shebang, Dukie."

"What's on your mind?"

"I just seen Jocko Henderson.

4

Hedgeway waved to Galleta. When his partner stepped out of the saloon the three men walked a few feet down the street and out of sight of the party. "Tell him, Si."

"I seen Jocko Henderson yesterday down the San Juan in that bend just north of the Mexican Hat."

"Was Tule with him? Or Anyone else?"

"Just Jocko. Drunk as a lord. I was down in the weeds making my mud when he rode by on the ridge line. He didn't see me. Hell he didn't even see my mule."

"Which way was he headed?"

"Hell if I know. I bet he don't neither. His horse was setting the direction."

Galleta looked at his partner. "Brodie. Are we to take him with us?"

"That's got to be his choice."

"I'll get him."

"Wait up a while and let him enjoy the party. We'll make preparations and then you can bust things up."

"Preparations for how many?"

"You and me. Brodie, we won't be able keep him away. Are you in, Si?"

"Callie Duphrane was always good to me. I'm in."

Galleta said, "Frenchy'll want in."

"All right. That's it then. Me and Si will get the supplies and horses. You talk to Frenchy. When we're ready, you can tell Brodie."

An hour later Galleta pulled Brodie to the side of the saloon and explained the situation.

Brodie listened and nodded. "Let's go."

Galleta put up his hand.

"Juan?"

"The girl, you damn fool." He shoved the young man back into the crowd.

Brodie walked to Enid cautiously, as if picking his way through a cholla forest.

She pretended, rather obviously, to be angry. "You left me, Mr. Duphrane. I should be angry."

"*Mister Duphrane?* What happened to Brodie?"

"I like the name Duphrane." Her eyes sparkled and a hint of a smile showed up in the corners of her lips. The smile faded quickly when he spoke.

"I have to go now, Enid."

"What on earth for? This is your party."

"Juan and Dukie and me have some business out of town. You're dad's going with us, old Si Vaughn, too."

Enid started to protest, but the stern look on Brodie's face blocked the effort. "Somebody's seen one of the men who killed your folks. That's what has happened, is it not?"

"Si Vaughn. He saw one of 'em up river."

"I don't suppose there is any way I can...."

He shook his head.

She stood on her tip toes and kissed him on the cheek, blushing at being so forward in public. "You be careful, Brodie."

About half the people in the saloon were watching, some out of the corners of their eyes and some without pretense. "Well, kiss her back, Brodie," shouted someone.

"I gotta go." Brodie blushed, turned and walked out of the saloon. He joined the others, mounted up and without words rode out of town. When he looked back, Enid was watching from outside the saloon. Young Adelson stood behind her.

Hedgeway took charge of the improvised posse as they headed north. Vaughn, the most experienced tracker, took the lead. "Si, you got any idea of where Jocko was headed?"

"That horse of his is dead, he just don't know it yet. He'll stick close to water. We'll find his tracks along the river."

"You sure?"

"Jocko was too drunk to hit the ground with his hat in three tries. He'll give that old horse the lead."

Hedgeway scanned the horizon, a flat land of ancient rivers towered over by tall mesas and broken by deep, rocky canyons and draws. "How the hell can we track him in all that?"

Vaughn laughed. "The same way we been tracking him the last half hour."

Brodie sat upright in his saddle. "Tracks?"

"It's Jocko all right. His horse is taking its time getting nowhere, and mighty wobbly at it."

Hedgeway leaned over and examine the ground. "I don't see any tracks."

"That's 'cause you ain't weasel smart like me. C'mon."

As they neared the river and the ground became softer, Hedgeway and the others were able to see the tracks Vaughn had been following. They crossed the river at a ford about sundown. "We may as well settle in here for the night boys. Ain't no use tracking in the dark."

They made camp, but did not build a fire. They shared biscuits and bacon and little conversation. Brodie barely spoke at all. Shortly after finishing their meal, Vaughn stood up. "I'm going to have a little looksee. Don't wait up."

An orange tinged deep blue sky soon turned black with the stars shining like sugar crystals on a black tablecloth. Brodie scooped the sand to make depressions fitting his shoulders and hips. He spread his blanket and was soon comfortably staring at the stars. Galleta followed his example. Hedgeway prepared his sleeping area the same way, but instead of bedding down walked to the edge of the campsite and settled into the darkness.

Hours later he drew his pistol as a shadow in the night caught his attention. He slowly cocked the .45 Colt, but to his ears the quiet click sounded like the slamming of a jailhouse door. The shadow moved toward the camp. Hedgeway holstered the pistol when he recognized Vaughn's thin frame.

"Vaughn. Over here," he whispered.

"Ain't no need to talk so low, Hedgeway. Jocko ain't nearby."

"We've lost him?"

"Hell no. C'mon." Vaughn led Hedgeway away from camp and to the top of a nearby ridgeline. The men paused a moment. The vastness of a broken land lit only by starlight was a powerful image even for those who lived among it. They drank it in.

"Yeah," Vaughn said.

"I know."

Vaughn waited another half moment and then pointed north. "Up there, on that butte. Look close there towards the far end. See it."

Hedgeway stared for a long moment. "Yeah. I see it."

A tiny yellow-gold flicker of light burst through the darkness, barely visible at times, but unmistakable.

"Campfire," Hedgeway said.

"It's got to be Jocko," Vaughn said.

A voice from several feet behind them said, "What are we waiting for."

Hedgeway and Vaughn turned quickly. Brodie stood in the shadows.

Hedgeway spit. "You know better than to sneak up on a man in the dark."

"I wasn't sneaking. You weren't paying attention."

Vaughn laughed. "He's got sand, that one."

Brodie joined the two men. "Like I said, what are we waiting for?"

Hedgeway said, "Some common sense, partner." He turned to Vaughn. "Can you get us up there in the dark?"

"I been there once or twice. It's a might twisty and thinner 'n a desert grasshopper in places, but, yessir. I can get us up there with both feet."

Hedgeway looked to the east. "False dawn is coming on. There's no way we can do that tonight. We'll hunker down tomorrow and make our move when the shadows start reaching out for a stretch. Agreed?"

22

"Agreed," Vaughn said.

Brodie nodded, and turned back to camp without saying a word.

Vaughn said, "You better keep an eye on the boy. If he gets gritty we could all end up dead."

5

The men didn't restrict their movements during the day; their staging area was out of sight of Henderson's camp. Each man checked his weapons. Vaughn carried a rebarreled 50.50 Spencer sporting rifle and a couple of Remington .44 revolvers. Hedgeway and Galetta carried .45 Colts. Brodie carried a double-action Smith and Wesson revolver. He cleaned it in the morning and repeated the process late in the afternoon, his eyes continually glancing up toward the distant butte. He finished and moved across the camp to sit down next to Galleta.

"How many times have you gone up against a man, Juan?"

"It is not something a man should count." He looked to something in the distance. "Many times during the Indian raids."

"You haven't ever… man to man?"

"No. Dukie, he has and many times. He was a young man in that Civil War of yours, a Texan then. He has looked into the eyes of a man he has just killed. He does not speak of it unless the whiskey loosens his tongue."

"I was just wondering."

"I advise you to avoid that subject with him. A man takes pride in battle, but not in the killing. It is strange, eh?"

"Like I said, I was just—"

"You will do fine, my new partner."

"Are you sure?"

"Do not think. Do not fear. Just do what you know how to do."

"That's just it; I don't rightly know what to do."

"When the moment arrives, you will know."

Vaughn had disappeared midday, leaving his mule in camp. Brodie watched him walk to the ridge, but lost him as the old man seemed to fade into the rocks. He knew Vaughn was crawling around up there, seeking a place to watch the trail to Henderson's camp, but he could see no movement, not even a slight spray of dust or the waving of tall grasses. Finally he gave up and went back to camp. The three men took turns keeping watch; one stayed on guard while the other two napped.

Brodie was on guard when he caught a movement from the ridge. Vaughn stepped out as if one of the rocks had suddenly taken life. His emergence was so quick that Brodie was startled. Vaughn walked quickly and arrived with a troubled look on his face.

"Jocko's got company. C'mon, let's deliver the bad news."

Vaughn explained the changing situation in camp. "I counted three riders headed up the trail to Jocko's camp. There's smoke rising from a campfire so they'll be cooking supper soon."

Hedgeway said, "That's good."

"What's good about it?" Brodie asked.

"Campfire smoke. They're not afraid of being seen. They don't know we're out here."

Galleta kicked the soft ground. "The element of surprise is a big advantage."

Hedgeway said, "Yeah, but there won't be any surprise. Even if we could sneak up to the base of that butte, they'd see us coming up that trail."

"They could pick us off by tumbling rocks on our heads," Brodie said.

Vaughn grinned.

Hedgeway said, "You know a back way up there don't you, you son of a bitch."

"That I do, gentlemen. That I do."

Vaughn grunted as he squatted down. The others followed suit as he drew lines in the sand. "This here's the butte and that's their camp on the far edge. Here's the trail they took up." He drew a zig zag line. "They can see us almost all the way." He stabbed a finger on the east end of the butte. "The other way is back here. It's a might skinny in parts and if you fall you got a good thousand foot trip to the last thing you'll ever see."

"A thousand feet." Brodie whistled.

Vaughn continued. "Yeah. Ain't no way our horses can make it. But we can. Once we get on top we just make our way down to their camp and… well, leave a free lunch for the coyotes."

Galleta looked to Hedgeway. "The law?"

"We're the law out here."

Galleta took a deep breath. "Agreed. Brodie, what do you say?"

"Yeah, but what about those other men?"

Vaughn said, "Bad company leads to bad ends."

Hedgeway nodded. "That's it, then. Si, we head out whenever you say."

Vaughn held his hand up, palm open to the sun. He moved it down in two stages. "Two hours until sundown. Be ready."

The sky was turning dark blue when he led them out of camp. They hugged the edge of the ridgeline, out of sight of Henderson's camp, and moved into a steeply-walled wash which took them near the eastern end of the butte. Vaughn scanned the area and waved them on. "They can't see us now, but move fast. Don't stop to sit and watch the paint dry."

They reached the base of the butte within a few moments, dismounted where Vaughn indicated, and hobbled their horses. The sky was dark, but starlight provided enough illumination to see well, provided they moved carefully. "It's all on foot from here on in, boys. The base of the trail's right here."

Brodie scanned the area. "I don't see any trail."

"You don't have to see it. Just follow me and do what I do."

McCutchen said, "What if you fall off?"

"Well, youngster, then you got options – fall or start flapping your wings. Let's git."

Vaughn moved out quickly. The others followed not so quickly. Hedgeway stepped up next, followed by Brodie, then McCutchen with Galleta bringing up the rear. The trail was just visible in the darkness, a pathway about two-feet wide at most and more rubble than road. Vaughn paused occasionally to allow the others to catch up.

Hedgeway said, "You're mighty sprightly for such an old fart."

"Clean living, sonny. You boys gonna be able to keep up?"

Brodie said, "We'll keep up, old man."

Vaughn chuckled, turned and moved out at a quick pace.

Hedgeway lightly shoved Brodie's shoulder. "Don't encourage him."

They continued climbing for several hours. The trail was a series of switchbacks and in places was no wider than a foot or so. Brodie looked over the edge to an ever-higher, steeper drop off with not tree or shrub to grab if he fell. A slip and fall would mean a fear filled, swift falling death – if he was lucky. If he was unlucky, he would fall, hit hard, and tumble down the slope breaking bones all the way and leaving his body too shattered to mend or to save. Death would come through the mercy of a friend's pistol, provided that friend could scramble down and find him. Brodie shook his head and focused on the steps immediately before him.

Later, when he looked ahead, he saw Vaughn helping Hedgeway up the final steps to the summit. Within moments the five men stood a thousand feet above the canyon floor. The faint lights of Goodridge and a few other small communities and even a few ranch houses were visible in all directions.

Brodie turned a full circle. "Damnation. It's like we're looking down on all creation."

Vaughn lifted his rifle off his back by the strap. "We got work to do, gentlemen."

Hedgeway said, "Where the hell's Henderson's camp from here?"

Vaughn pointed south. "Traveling's pretty easy from here on in if you watch your step. The only hard part is a little drop off above where they throwed down their blankets. Mind where you put your toes and you'll be all right."

"What is our plan," Galleta said.

"I've been thinking some on that," McCutchen said.

Vaughn cleared his throat. "There ain't but one plan and you know it."

Brodie spoke in a low voice, although they were at least a mile from Henderson's camp. "Somebody tell me just what the hell that plan is."

Hedgeway, too, spoke in a low voice. "They're not going to let us take 'em prisoner. That means they're going to put up a fight."

"Ambush is the only way, sonny," Vaughn said.

"Agreed," Hedgeway said. He looked over to Galleta.

"Si."

McCutchen said, "Wish I did, but I don't see any other sensible way."

"You didn't ask my opinion," Brodie said.

"I don't have to. I've seen you practicing with that pistol of yours. You've been waiting for this a long time."

Brodie nodded. "Henderson is mine."

Vaughn said, "Look, sonny, this ain't no vendetta ride. This is strictly a corpse and cartridge situation. We shoot everybody. One of us will get him. Might even be you."

"I'll get him." Brodie's face took on an uncommon hard and angry expression.

Vaughn put his hand on the young man's shoulder. "You got to be quietner 'n a hole in the ground to do what we're about."

Brodie nodded and the men moved on.

Vaughn led them to the drop off above Henderson's camp within an hour. The four men sat around a fire. The smell of burning pinion pine filled the air as the smoke rose and mingled with the stars. They passed a bottle around and were talking loudly.

Vaughn motioned his comrades back from the edge. He waved them in close and whispered. "There's a narrow slot over yonder, a break in the rocks. We can slip through there one at a time. "Me first then you, Dukie. Juan and Frenchy next, and Brodie, you bring up the rear."

"But I—," Brodie said.

Vaughn said, "We all got the same chance at getting Henderson no matter where we stand."

"We all have the same shot, Brodie," Hedgeway said.

"All right. I'll go last."

Vaughn pointed to the dark slot. "I'll sneak around some place on the east end of the ledge. Dukie you pick a spot somewhere north of me. Frenchy, you pick a spot somewhere in the middle of what's going to happen. Juan move to the far west side and Brodie, you find yourself a spot on the far end near that ledge. When you're in position, get ready 'cause I'm going to open one of 'em up like a can of beans."

"How are you going to know we're in position," Brodie said.

"You ain't so all fired quiet as you boys think. Just hope Jocko and his pals is too tied up with that tangle-leg whiskey to listen for what they ought to be listening for. Let's git." He took a step and then stopped and turned to Brodie. "If you can spot Jocko, he's yours. But don't waste time picking out targets. When you see a man, you kill a man."

"I'll hold up my end."

Vaughn led them to the slot, a narrow crack about two-feet wide angling steeply down to the level ground below. Vaughn moved slowly over the rubble, doing his best to stop a noisy rock slide. The old man was skillful and he made it the thirty or so feet down without making a noise. He waved Hedgeway on and walked away.

The other three followed, moving even slower and with more care. They fanned out to their assigned positions. Henderson's camp was on a flat rock area at the edge of a drop off. Their horses were tied among a group of pinion pines jutting out of the rock and the yellow-brown dust. Brodie worked his way around to a couple of barrel sized boulders under a low hanging pinion, a perfect place for an ambush. He had an unobstructed view of the camp with minimal exposure to return fire in the unlikely event they ever saw him. He glanced around. The camp was at the very edge of the butte. A long narrow ledge jutted out to the west. Someone might survive the initial assault, but an escape to the ledge would lead only to a dead end and a long fall to the canyon floor. Henderson and his men were trapped.

Brodie recognized Jocko Henderson immediately. He pulled the Smith and Wesson from its holster and cocked the hammer. He took a deep breath and then took aim. His face was emotionless as he remembered something Juan Galleta had said to him many years before.

"Never smile and shoot, my young friend. It breeds an evil nature."

"Vaughn, it's time. Start the party, damn it. Shoot." he whispered.

On the other side of the camp Vaughn opened the breech of the Spencer and inserted a cartridge. He closed the breech, cocking the hammer, raised his rifle to his shoulder and sighted in the back of a large man bent over near the fire. He held his breath. Before he could pull the trigger, the man leaned quickly to his side, spoiling the shot. Vaughn waited, but the man stood up and stretched. He scratched his privates, said something Vaughn couldn't hear, and walked away from the firelight and into the darkness. Vaughn lowered his rifle. *Take your time, youngster. I got all night*, he thought.

Across the ledge the man scratched his privates again and half-walked half-stumbled out of the firelight and into the darkness. He stepped up to a couple of low boulders beneath a pinion tree and unbuttoned his britches. He reached inside the flap, but stopped when he noticed two eyes staring at him from behind the boulders. He blinked and rubbed his red, runny eyes. He never heard the gunshot that put a bullet through his head. He fell onto the boulders, partially blocking Brodie's view of the camp. Brodie stepped out, protected only by the darkness and took aim.

Gunfire exploded all around the camp as Vaughn, Hedgeway, Galleta and McCutchen opened fire.

Two of the men around the fire jumped for the shadows. The other stood up and started kicking sand into the flames. He was the second man to die that night. Vaughn's shot ripped through his chest and another shot by Hedgeway tore into the man's gut. He fell onto the remnants of the fire and his blood steamed on the hot coals.

Slowly, the night became quiet and dark. The two men who had jumped into the shadows had moved in different directions and were separated. Vaughn thought, *Like I said, boys, we got all night.* He leaned back against a rock and waited.

Brodie looked down on the man he had just killed. The dead man faced upward, but it wasn't the face of Jocko Henderson. He replaced the empty shell in his revolver with a live round and waited.

Moments passed with only the sound of a heavy breeze through the trees. A slight sound caught his attention – rocks slipping under someone's feet. Somewhere nearby McCutchen was moving in. A dry twig snapped and three shots blazed from the darkness near the edge of the drop off. One of the shells ricocheted and smacked into a tree just down from Brodie's position. Brodie slipped down behind the protection of the boulders.

"Mr. McCutchen, are you all right?"

"Yeah!" The voice was wobbly.

Someone shouted from the darkness, one of the men trapped on the ledge. "What the hell do you bastards want?"

Vaughn's voice shot through the night air. "Jocko Henderson."

"He ain't here."

Vaughn laughed and fired a shot into the night. "I know your voice, Jocko."

Three shots exploded the darkness, all three aimed toward Vaughn's position. Hedgeway and Galleta returned fire. Hedgeway shouted, "We got all night, boys. And you got no way to go but down."

One of the three trapped men fired another round.

Hedgeway shouted, "Juan, everybody, settle in and get comfortable. We'll wait 'em out."

"Si," shouted Galleta.

"Yo," shouted McCutchen.

Neither Brodie nor Vaughn responded.

Hedgeway shouted, "Brodie, Si – don't you boys do nothing crazy. Daylight's coming. We'll pick 'em off then."

Two more shots lit up the darkness near the ledge. Brodie noticed the position of the nearest shooter. The starlight exposed a winding lane of spruce and pinion. He squatted down for a better look. The ground between him and the shooter was more sand than rock. *He'll never hear me*, Brodie thought. He eased away from the protection of the boulders and moved forward slowly and in a crouch and always keeping a tree between him and the place where he believed one of the shooters to be.

His boots made no sound in the soft sand, but he moved forward slowly and with great care. A dry twig, just buried under the sand snapped. Brodie leaped to his right and rolled on the ground, crawling behind a low boulder. Two shots from the darkness ahead kicked up the sand where he had been walking.

Two more shots flashed from behind and to his left – Hedgeway or Galleta or perhaps both had fired. Brodie used the few seconds he knew he had to scramble behind a mound of sand piled up beneath a pinion pine. *Maybe I will wait until sun up.* He glanced to the east and the gray blue light that marked false dawn. In another hour or so, the butte would be in full sunlight. *I got time, Henderson. Yours is about all up.*

When the bright yellow glow burst over the far mountains and started a glow in the rocky, red landscape, Brodie resisted the urge to watch the spectacular play of retreating shadows. To his south he could see the sunlight striking the dramatic landscape men were beginning to call Monument Valley. His eyes darted away from the distant scenery to the danger at hand. A man was sprawled out in the open less than twenty yards ahead. The amount of red blood that had soaked into the yellow sand meant that the man had been dead since the last shots were fired.

"One down over here," he shouted.

"Two to go," shouted Hedgeway.

A single shot rang out and a man near the edge stood and grabbed at his shirt. He tore it away as if desperate to find some treasure. Another shot ripped into his shoulder and he staggered back. He turned as if trying to escape, but his legs wouldn't obey his orders and he fell.

"Only, one now, Amigo," shouted Galleta.

Hedgeway shouted, "Jocko Henderson!"

"Yeah." The voice came from near the edge of the cliff.

"How do you want it? A bullet here or a rope in town?"

A moment passed.

"Henderson!"

"I surrender."

"Come on out."

"Can't. I'm hit in the leg. You boys come get me. I'll go peaceful."

McCutchen stepped out from behind a scrub brush. Henderson popped up from a wide crack in the surface of the butte, twisted slightly and took aim.

Brodie fired. The bullet slammed into Henderson's shoulder. He dropped his gun and fell back. Hedgeway and Galleta jumped from their positions and were standing over the man within seconds. Brodie walked over at a leisurely pace. Henderson was wedged down in a crack in the butte's surface a few feet from the drop off. Hedgeway pulled him up. The man grunted in pain and cursed his captors. Galleta checked him for hidden weapons and pulled a small .32 caliber single-shot pistol from beneath his vest and an old Green River knife from his boot. He threw the knife and then the pistol over the edge of the cliff. Henderson looked over his shoulder as they fell. The weapons were out of sight long before they hit the ground some 1,000 feet or more below.

Henderson held his shoulder. The wound looked painful, but it was obviously not mortal. "All right, you sons of bitches, take me in." His body swayed slightly, but his face showed only anger and contempt.

Galleta looked to Brodie, but he spoke to Henderson. "That is a matter for your judge."

"I got rights," Henderson said.

Hedgeway said, "Shut up."

"You said—"

"I said shut up."

McCutchen looked to Hedgeway. "What are you doing?"

"Stepping aside."

Galleta grabbed McCutchen's arm and pulled him away. "Come on, amigo. We should go share a smoke with our friend Vaughn."

"I...."

"Amigo." McCutchen looked back, a confused look on his face. He turned and followed Galleta up toward Vaughn's position.

Hedgeway kept his pistol pointed at Henderson's chest. "Brodie, you got anything to say?"

Brodie stepped up and stood face-to-face with Henderson. "Do you remember me?"

"No."

"The Duphrane place, down near the Mexican hat. Years ago. You made me watch—"

"The kid... the stupid kid."

Hedgeway said, "He ain't no kid anymore."

Henderson looked closely at Brodie and a look of recognition crossed his face. "You take after your daddy... he was a gutless coward."

If Henderson was expecting to get an emotional response he was disappointed.

"That's about the size of it," Hedgeway said. He put his pistol in its holster. "I'm going to grab a smoke with Si." He turned quickly and walked away.

Brodie kept his pistol pointed at the man's gun. "You raped and murdered my mother."

Henderson smiled, a sick and twisted grin. "I remember your momma, too." His smile grew broader. "What a waste of baby juice."

Brodie stood motionless for a moment, just staring at the man. He put his pistol back in its holster and stepped forward.

6

Hedgeway, Galleta and McCutchen stood above Si Vaughn who was on the ground and leaning against a rock. All four were smoking. More than a quarter of an hour had passed since they left Brodie and Henderson at the edge of the drop off.

"There," Galleta said.

Brodie walked toward them at a leisurely pace. When he arrived Hedgeway spoke. "Henderson?"

"He tripped."

Hedgeway held out a small pouch of tobacco. Brodie shook his head. "What's wrong with Si?"

Vaughn smiled weakly and pointed to the left side of his chest. "Took one last night."

"Hell, why didn't you call for help?"

"I didn't want to take another."

Brodie squatted down.

McCutchen put his hand on the young man's shoulder. "We've already done everything we can."

"I'm sorry you got involved in all this, old man," Brodie said.

"It's a small price to pay for a cleaner smelling world. I always hated them Henderson boys."

"We'll get you back to town and—"

"No, you won't."

Hedgeway kneeled down next to Brodie. "The kid's right, Si. Maybe—"

"There ain't no maybe. I'm going under. That bullet tore the hell out of my insides. I wouldn't even make it down...."

Vaughn coughed, the effort causing spasms of pain.

McCutchen said, "We can't just leave him here."

"The hell you can't," Vaughn said. He coughed again before speaking. "You got some burying to do over there. I ain't going to die with them varmints stinking up my funeral."

Brodie sat down. "I'll stay with him."

Hedgeway led the others back toward the camp and the dead men. They dragged the bodies in and lined them up.

"I don't see a shovel," McCutchen said.

"I'm not surprised," Hedgeway said.

Galleta squatted down and grabbed a fist full of sand. He let it drop and blow away in the wind. "What we bury the wind will expose soon. It is a waste of effort."

McCutchen said, "We can't just leave 'em. I mean, with Si over there and all."

Galleta thought for a moment and then grabbed one of the dead men by his boots and dragged him to the edge of the cliff. He placed his foot against the man's chest and rolled him over the side. He crossed himself afterward. Hedgeway and McCutchen looked at each other, nodded and followed Galleta's example.

The three men stood at the edge, but the bodies were so far below they couldn't be seen among the rocks. McCutchen took off his hat. "Shouldn't we say something?"

Hedgeway leaned over the edge. "Yeah." He spit, turned and walked away. "I'll get their horses." The other two looked down again and turned back to the camp. Within moments the wind had kicked up enough sand to cover the blood on the ground. It was as if the men had never existed.

Si was alert and showing only a moderate amount of pain when they returned. Brodie had done all he could to make the old man comfortable. He had crafted a shady spot by ramming a couple of pinion limbs into the earth and topping it with a blanket he had draped over the boulder at Si's back. He steadied the entire construction with carefully placed rocks.

"Thanks, boy."

Hedgeway returned with the horses. McCutchen stepped over and took their reins. "I'll watch these… if you want to say something."

"Thanks." He walked over and stood with the others. Their faces were grim.

Vaughn looked up. "Hell, boys, I ain't gone under yet."

Galleta kneeled down and patted the old man on his knee. "I will see you again, amigo… on the other side." He stood up quickly and walked away.

Vaughn looked up to Hedgeway. "I got something to say to the boy."

Hedgeway spoke to Brodie. "We'll go on ahead. Catch up when you can."

"He won't be long," Vaughn said.

"Silas…."

"I know, Dukie. Now, git."

Hedgeway joined the others and led them away. Vaughn coughed and fought for breath. When the spasm ended he jerked on a leather thong around his neck and retrieved a small leather pouch. He opened it and pulled out a ceramic smoking pipe. The stem was broken near tip. "Damn. I bought that in New Orleans; lasted ten years it did." He pulled something rolled in paper from the pouch and then filled the bowl with tobacco, also from the pouch. He handed the paper to Brodie. "You mind doing the honors?"

"Sure thing, Si." Brodie unrolled the paper, pulled out a match and struck it against the boulder. He held the flame over Vaughn's pipe.

"Thanks, son." He closed his eyes and enjoyed the smoke.

"Why did you want me to hold back, Si?"

"I want to warn you 'gainst something, Brodie. You got a taste of blood today. That affects a man."

"Yes, Sir. I think it must." He glanced quickly over to the rim and then back.

"Some men get a bit queasy about that sort of thing, thinking Saint Pete ain't going to consider 'em a candidate for a pair of wings."

"I'm not proud of what we did here, Si. But I'm not ashamed either."

"That's kind a' what I'm getting at. Some fellers take to that taste of blood. They get to where they need it."

"That's not me, Si."

"Good, Brodie. Now...." Vaughn coughed. He dropped his pipe, spilling the contents. Brodie picked it up, refilled and lit it and handed it to the old man.

"You're a good man, Brodie. I'd like to shake your hand."

They shook hands. Vaughn's grip was still powerful. He took another drag from his pipe and looked away. "Go on, now. Go marry that girl they was talking about and get that stork flying into your cabin."

"I can't just leave you hear, Si."

"Hell, son. Look." He pointed out to the vast open space below. "Can you think of a better place?"

"I...."

"Go on, Brodie. I got to rope a cloud and...." He broke into a coughing spasm. "Git."

Brodie stood up. He double checked the shelter and moved on. The pleasant odor of smoking tobacco followed on the wind as he moved to catch up with his companions. As he stepped over the small rise he heard a faint click. It could have been a loose rock, but to Brodie it sounded like a ceramic pipe falling on rocky ground.

7

The next year passed without incident. The townsfolk voted to change the name of their tiny community to Mexican Hat. A few more stores opened, one of them a dress shop run by Enid McCutchen. The HGD Ranch grew in size if not in profits. And Brodie invested much of the little free time he had visiting Enid McCutchen.

"When are you going to marry that girl of yours, Brodie?"

Hedgeway grabbed the other end of the heavy pole Brodie held in his hands and lifted. They placed it between two upright posts and nailed it into position, finishing the corral they had been working on all day. Hedgeway placed his hands on the railing and gave it a shake. "She'll do." He glanced to the west where the sun was just dipping below the far mesa on the horizon. He took off his work gloves and sniffed the air. "Steak. The Earl's timing is just about right – as usual. Steak tonight."

"I hope he's cooked up some taters to go with it."

"About Enid...."

"Yeah?"

"It's been more 'n a year since we made you a partner. Ain't it about time we built a little cabin for two over by the shade tree?"

"I'm thinking on it."

"Thinking's a sure fire way to start losing. Young Adelson's been giving her the eye lately."

Brodie grunted. "A man's got a responsibility to afford a wife."

"You *afford* a soiled dove, my friend. You earn a wife."

"That's just it. I'm not earning near enough. We're barely holding our own with the ranch and I only got a few hundred dollars saved up. I need—"

"A flower like Enid McCutchen will soon grace someone's home. You had best stop thinking and start proposing."

"I believe in treating a woman right."

"So does young Adelson."

They walked back toward the ranch house, their pace picking up as they got closer and the smell of roasting meat became stronger. They stopped at the front door. A washbasin and towel sat on a bench. First Hedgeway and then Brodie washed their faces and hands.

"Damnation," Brodie said.

"The Earl is mighty particular about such things."

"We didn't have to make such a fuss when Juan was the cook."

"We didn't eat so good either."

Hedgeway stepped inside. Brodie followed. Galleta sat at the dinner table. Earl Lawrence Plowright, a tall and thin man wearing a well-worn dress coat stood at the head of the table. He spoke with a British accent. "Gentlemen, I shall have dinner served within moments." He bowed his head slightly, turned and moved into the kitchen area just across the room. He returned with a large plate piled high with steaks and potatoes. A moment later he poured each man a cup of coffee and then stood off to the side of the table.

Galleta cut into his steak and looked to Plowright. "Sit and eat with us, Earl."

"It would not be proper, sir."

Hedgeway spoke through a mouth full of potato. "Hell, man, we freed the slaves ages ago. Sit down."

Plowright looked to the ceiling.

Brodie said, "Sit down and eat, Earl. This isn't England; it's Utah."

"Proper etiquette is not restricted to—"

"You sit down and eat or I won't get that apple pie recipe from Enid for you."

"Very well, sir." Plowright sat down. A place setting was already on the table. Galleta forked over a steak while Brodie stabbed a potato and dropped it on Earl's plate.

Hedgeway grinned. "The Earl is in rare form tonight. What's the occasion?"

Plowright cleared his throat. "I shall be visiting Mrs. Knauss this evening. After my evening labors are completed, of course."

"Of course." He swallowed and sipped his coffee. "Take Brodie with you. Teach him something about courting – Britisher style."

The widow Knauss owned and operated a general merchandise store, a very successful business. Enid McCutchen rented a small space for her dress shop in the back, so Brodie and Plowright had a common destination.

They rode in silence for a short while before Brodie said, "You ever think about going back to England?"

"I hardly know the place."

"But that's your country."

"I served in Her Majesty's forces twenty years – Africa, India, back to Africa. I rarely saw the land of my birth." He swept his arm in a wide ark. "This is my country."

"Do you plan on staying on with us, as a cook I mean?"

"That, sir, entirely depends upon the attitude of the widow Knauss."

"She's coming around to your way of thinking, is she?"

"With apologies to Mr. Shakespeare, Brodie, I shall woo her, I shall wed her and I shall most assuredly bed her."

"I love the way you talk, Earl. I surely do."

The only businesses still open in Mexican Hat were the saloons, so the duo split up. The widow Knauss owned a nice house at the edge of town. Plowright stopped there while Brodie rode on through to the McCutchen place at the opposite end of town. After the usual pleasantries with her family, she and Brodie went for a walk to go window shopping.

Brodie scratched his head in an exaggerated manner. "Window shopping. Enid, you work in those windows all day."

"It's not the same. Besides, I wanted us to have a little time to ourselves."

"Yes, Ma'am."

He took her arm and edged her across the street and avoiding a walk past Adelson's Livery. Enid smiled, but said nothing about the change in direction. As they neared the far edge of town they saw a buggy coming down the road, a lone woman behind the reins. They watched as she passed by. The woman stared at them, her eyes seemingly focused on Brodie for a moment. She stopped in town at the livery stable. Young Adelson came out and the two began talking. Brodie nudged Enid on.

"Do you know that woman," he said.

"I've never seen her before."

"Odd, a woman traveling alone, especially this time of day."

"She seemed worried, frightened even."

Plowright and Knauss were on the front porch of the widow's home. The older couple exchanged a few quiet words and then Plowright waved them in. Within moments they were engaged in polite conversation, much of it concerning the sudden arrival of the woman in the buggy.

"I am most confident that the ladies of Mexican Hat, with their inevitable network of spies and informants, shall clear up the mystery by the morrow," Plowright said.

Knauss slapped him on his arm.

"It is true, Madam."

"Then there is no call for discussing the obvious, Mr. Plowright," she said.

The conversation continued for a long time before Enid said she needed to return home. Through a pre-arranged signal, Plowright suggested that Brodie return to the ranch on his own. Enid caught sight of the slight smile on his face and smiled a bit herself as they left.

They were halfway to the McCutchen place when Brodie suddenly stopped. He grabbed her arm so she was forced to stop also. "Do you hear that?"

"What?"

Brodie cocked his head. "Christ!" He let go of Enid's hand. "Go home. Send your pa back. Hurry."

"What is—"

"Now!"

Brodie turned and ran to the end of the store and rushed into the narrow alley between two buildings. The sound was a woman screaming, her voice muffled, but unmistakable. When he reached the rear of the building he saw the woman who had passed by earlier. She was being beaten by two rough looking saddle bums. One held her arms behind her back with one hand. The other hand covered her mouth. She kicked savagely at the man beating her, but he easily dodged her efforts. She was far less lucky. He hit her three terrible blows in rapid succession.

Brodie screamed. "No!" Blind rage took command and he rushed in and tackled the man who had been striking the woman. The men rolled in the sand, Brodie punching with all his strength against a man older and larger than himself. The man tried to back off, but Brodie kept punching.

The other man threw the woman aside. He pulled his pistol and rushed to the fight and hit Brodie on the side of the head. Brodie waivered a second and then fell over into the sand. He struggled to get on all fours as the two assailants approached.

8

The larger of the two men kicked Brodie in the ribs. "Let's get out of here." The men backed away, ignoring the woman, mounted their horses and rode into the darkness. Brodie crawled to the woman.

"Are you all right, Ma'am?"

She looked at him, but her eyes were wide and uncomprehending. She tried to speak, but could only rasp out bits and pieces of words that made no sense. Frenchy McCutchen appeared at the corner of the alley, a Winchester in hand. After a fast survey of the scene, he rushed to Brodie and the woman.

"Is she all right?"

Brodie brushed the hair from her face. The scratches and bruises did not disfigure her beauty. "I don't know. You'd better get Doc Palmer."

McCutchen took time to look around. No one else was in sight. "You sure?"

"Whoever did this is long gone."

"I'll be right back." He handed over the rifle. "Just in case."

"Sure."

McCutchen hurried away. Brodie turned his attention to the mystery woman. "How bad are you hurt, Ma'am? Can you understand me?"

She blinked several times as if trying to focus not only her vision, but also her thoughts. Her expression turned to fear and she tried to scramble away. "I won't tell you anything." Her voice was weak.

She kicked out at Brodie. He spread his arms wide and eased back. "You're with friends, Ma'am. I'm not going to hurt you."

Still on the ground, she moved back a few feet. Brodie stayed in place and kept his arms wide. She looked around, her eyes wide with fear. "It's my secret, my gold. You'll get nothing from me." She picked up a small rock and held it as a weapon.

Brodie lowered his arms and forced a smile. "You hold on to that rock. I'll just keep my hands on this here Winchester.

She paused a few seconds and then dropped the rock. "You're not one of them, are you?" Speaking seemed to require a great effort.

"No, Ma'am. I more or less chased 'em off. I sent for our doctor. You're going to be all right."

"I don't think so."

The woman fainted. He rushed to her side just as McCutchen and Doc Palmer arrived. Palmer made a brief examination. "I think we can safely move her."

McCutchen said, "Take her to my place. We have that spare room."

Palmer's office was nearby. He sent McCutchen to bring back blankets so they could make a stretcher. Within minutes she was in the McCutchen's spare room where Palmer began a more thorough examination. After he finished he joined the family and Brodie around the kitchen table.

"Brodie, do you know this woman?"

"I never saw her before tonight."

Enid refilled his coffee cup. "She rode in pretty hard and left her rig at Adelson's place. She looked scared to me."

"It looks like she had good reason," Palmer said.

Brodie said, "How is she, Doc?"

"She's scratched, cut and bruised pretty badly, but nothing to serious. She ought to be responding better."

"What do you mean," Brodie said.

"Her wounds are superficial. I'm afraid there may be internal injuries."

"What can we do," Enid said.

"Not much, really... keep her still... wait and see."

McCutchen scratched his chin. "She can stay here until you say she can go."

"That's awfully generous, Frenchy. And pretty much what I expected." He turned his attention to Brodie. "How about you?"

"They got in a couple of good licks, but I'm all right."

Palmer finished his coffee and stood up. "I'll check in on her tomorrow. But come get me immediately if her condition goes south."

Later, when Brodie was about to leave, McCutchen refused to let Enid see him off. He escorted the younger man outside. "I know what you're thinking, Brodie, and I advise against it."

"What do you think I'm thinking?"

"You'll never track those men in the dark. Besides, they have one hell of a head start on you."

"They beat a woman, Mr. McCutchen. Nearly beat her to death."

"And they got away with it. For now."

"I can't let something like that go."

"You can. Like I said, for now. Let's let that woman heal up and see what she has to say before you ride off on some kind of vengeance trail."

"That isn't so easy for somebody like me." Brodie stepped into the stirrup and eased into the saddle.

"You need to start using more of your head and less of your heart." McCutchen patted the flank of Brodie's horse. "Besides, if you run off and get yourself killed, I'll have to put up with Adelson's kid hanging around here. I can't stand that little pup."

Brodie smiled. "All right, Mr. McCutchen."

"You can call me Frenchy, you know."

"Yes, Sir."

"Go on, now. You have a ranch to run. The good Lord will take care of those men in His own good time."

Brodie nodded and headed toward the edge of town. McCutchen watched him for a moment and then went inside. As Brodie neared the widow Knauss's place he turned and rode back to the scene of the fight. He rode to the edge of the faint light cast from the town and looked into the darkness. Eventually he sighed and turned toward the road and his ranch.

9

Brodie, Hedgeway and Galleta rotated cooking and cleaning up chores and it was Brodie's week as the domestic. After breakfast the youngest of the trio busied himself washing dishes. When he finished and stepped outside he saw his partners conversing under a large cottonwood a couple of hundred yards from the ranch house. He walked toward them and as he approached, Hedgeway made a big show of stepping off a straight line out from the tree. He stopped and rammed a stick into the earth, turned and stepped off again at a 90 degree angle.

"What's he doing, Juan?"

"Measuring for the cabin."

"Cabin?"

"Si."

"What do we need a cabin for?"

"Quiet or I will lose count."

"Dukie's the one doing the pacing off."

"Today I am foreman. I do the counting."

"Just what is—"

"Shhh!"

Hedgeway finished marching off a square. He paused and looked back as if examining some great work and then joined his partners. "That'll do."

"Why are you men wanting a cabin here?"

Hedgeway said, "It's for Enid."

Brodie blushed. "I'm not ready to—"

Galleta said, "We did not say for *you* and Enid."

Hedgeway said, "Me and Juan are going into town and see which one of us can lasso that gal proper."

"You're crazy."

"The man who does not marry that senorita is the crazy one."

Brodie sighed. "I can't even afford to set her up in a decent house."

"You're a decent man, Brodie. That's all she really needs."

"Even if you are something of a fool, amigo."

Hedgeway pointed the way back toward the ranch house. "That load of lumber ought to be in by now. I'll hitch up the wagon and—"

"I'll go," Brodie said.

He rushed off to the barn to the sound of laughter from his partners.

Brodie's first stop in town was to pick up the lumber, which he loaded with remarkable speed. He saw Doc Palmer stepping out of his office. The man waved him down and hitched a ride. "I figure you're headed over to see Enid," he said.

"Good figuring, Doc."

"Drop me off at the McCutchen place."

A touch of impatience crept into Brodie's voice. "It's just down the street, Doc. Walking distance."

"I want to speak with you about something."

"All right, what?"

"Jess."

"Who's Jess?"

"That woman you saved. She finally started talking – a bit. It seems her name is Jess, Jess Belle Cutler, she says."

"Funny name."

"And probably not her real name. But...."

They arrived at the McCutchen residence before Palmer could explain himself. Mrs. McCutchen stepped out, greeted and invited them in. "I'll fix us a pot of coffee," she said.

"Brodie, I know you're chomping at the bit to go see Enid, but stick around until I'm through. All right?"

"Okay, Doc. But can you make it quick?"

Palmer shook his head. "No. But I won't be all that long. Just wait."

Brodie and Mrs. McCutchen made small talk while Palmer stepped into the spare room to examine his latest patient. When he finished, he stepped out and accepted a cup of coffee. He sat down at the table.

Mrs. McCutchen said, "What is your verdict, Doctor?"

"She appears to be terribly weak, but I can't say why for sure. Perhaps one of her ribs has punctured a lung, but that's just a guess."

"Will she be... will she recover?"

"I think so, given time."

"This is a good Christian house, Doctor. We will gladly allow her to stay until she is recovered."

Ma'am, you are truly building up treasures in heaven."

Brodie noticed his toe tapping on the wooden floorboard. He forced his foot down. A forced smile required more effort. Mrs. McCutchen seemed to be enjoying his discomfort. "Enid will be happy to see you, Brodie. That is, if you plan on stopping by her shop on your way back to the ranch."

"Yes, Ma'am. I'd like to say hello."

"She will be delighted to see you. More coffee, Doctor?"

Palmer nodded and Brodie's toe started tapping again. Mrs. McCutchen stifled a chuckle. Later, Palmer finished his coffee and stood up. "Well, I must go. Thank you for the hospitality, Mrs. McCutchen. I will check in on our patient tomorrow."

"Does she need anything special?"

"Keep her drinking plenty of water. Get her to eat more if you can. Help her with the... ah, necessarium if required." Mrs. McCutchen blushed, but nodded her head. "Brodie, let's go."

"About time. I mean, ah, thank you for the coffee, Ma'am."

They left quickly. Palmer climbed on the wagon.

"Doc, your office is right over there."

Brodie ignored the hint. "When you saved that woman, how badly was she beaten?"

"You know that better than I do."

"From your point of view, how bad?"

"They roughed her up pretty good."

"Did you notice if they, well, did they just work on her abdomen… her stomach?"

Brodie flicked the reins and the wagon moved into the street. "No. The guy doing all the hitting was all over the place."

"Did you see them force anything down her throat?"

"What are you getting at?"

"I'm grasping at straws. Could they have poisoned the woman?"

Brodie stopped the wagon in front of Palmer's office. "I don't think so, Doc. I mean, she fought back like a wildcat. She didn't look poisoned to me. I sure didn't see anything like that."

"Curious."

"How's that?"

"Her wounds are very superficial. Oh, she'll have some bruises for a few weeks and the scratches will heal without scars. But she's not recovering as she should."

"Those infernal injuries you talked about."

"Internal, Brodie, internal. And I don't know." He hopped off the wagon. "Tell Enid I said hello."

Brodie drove the team of mules further down the street and pulled the wagon behind Knauss Mercantile. Enid stepped out the back door and tossed a washbasin of water into the dirt. The sun caught her hair flying in the gentle breeze. Her eyes sparkled and when she saw Brodie she smiled.

Brodie stepped off the wagon. "I ain't crazy."

10

Several days later a rider from town rode into the HGD Ranch, a kid who worked part time for Adelson's Livery. He saw Brodie working on the gate at the corral and rode over.

"Mr. Duphrane, I got a message for you."

"Who from?"

"The McCutchens."

"Enid?"

"All of 'em. They said they want you to come in as soon as you can."

"Is anybody in trouble? Hurt?"

"No, at least I don't think so. They just said for you to get into town muy pronto."

"Tell 'em I'll be there shortly."

"You bet." The kid rode away and Brodie walked to the ranch house. He cleaned up quickly and left a note on the table for his partners. Half an hour later he tied his horse to the railing outside the McCutchen place. Frenchy sat on the porch, smoking his pipe. He stood up when Brodie stepped through the weathered picket fence.

"Come on in, Brodie. She's asking for you."

"Enid? Is she all right?"

"Enid's fine. It's Jess. She's been asking for you something fierce. Come on."

He led Brodie inside. Enid and Mrs. McCutchen sat at the kitchen table. Mrs. McCutchen said, "She's been asking for you all morning."

"I'd best see what she wants." He paused. "One of you ought to go with me. It wouldn't be proper otherwise."

Frenchy sat down at the table. "Enid, you go. She seems fond of you."

A moment later Brodie and Enid sat down beside Jess Belle Cutler. The woman's bruises and scratches were practically healed and she looked healthy.

"What can I do for you, Ma'am?"

"You've done so much already. You saved my life."

"Any man around here would have done the same."

"But you're the man who did. I want to repay you."

"That's not necessary."

Cutler sat up in bed. The effort seemed to cause her some discomfort. Enid helped her arrange a pillow behind her back for support. She finished and backed away, standing close to Brodie.

"Unless those two men beat me crazy, it seems to me that you two are headed for the matrimonial yoke."

Enid blushed and Brodie turned his head slightly away.

Cutler smiled. "I knew it."

Brodie said, "We haven't exact—"

"I want to give you two something to build on – if you ain't... if you are not afraid of hard work and more than a little danger."

Enid said, "Miss Cutler, Jess, what on earth are you talking about?"

"Gold."

Enid's eyes lit up.

Brodie frowned. "Begging your pardon, Ma'am, but you don't seem to be what I'd call a wealthy woman."

Cutler laughed and then coughed. Enid poured her a glass of water. She continued, "I should say hidden gold, down in New Mexico. We can share it."

"I'm a rancher, Miss Cutler."

"A struggling rancher would be my guess. Help me get that gold and you can buy half the ranches in Utah."

"I appreciate that and all, but...."

"Think about Enid, Mr. Duphrane. Think about her life as it's going to be. And then think about her life as it could be."

Brodie leaned forward. He looked to Enid and then back to Cutler. "I'll listen, but I don't make any promises."

Cutler placed her hand on Enid's hand and squeezed gently. "You listen. And you dream while I talk." She looked to Brodie. "Years ago some miners north of Lordsburg high-graded a lot of ore. It took 'em more than a year. They built an arrastra, ground it up and separated the gold from the dust. They had bags of the stuff all of it hidden up someplace south of the Gila."

"That's Apache country," Brodie said.

"So, you can figure out what happened to them... those miners."

"The army found what was left of them over around a place they call Red Rock."

Enid said, "The gold?"

"Lost. All the miners were tortured and killed."

Enid said, "I don't understand."

Cutler sat up straighter and pointed to her bags in the corner of the room. "Open the canvas bag and bring me the leather case."

Brodie did as she indicated. She opened the case and pulled out a faded square of paper covered in various markings. "They made a map of where they hid the gold. One of the Apaches had been a scout for the Army and he knew the value of markings on paper. He kept the map. Later he met some soldier, scout, rancher or somebody he trusted and asked him to read what was on the paper. The man he trusted killed him on the spot."

"And you have the map," Brodie said.

"I have part of it; half to exact, but I know who has the other half." Enid's voice quavered. She paused to catch her breath. "That's the danger part." She was still looking at Brodie.

Brodie sat down on a chair near the window. "And you know where this man is?"

"He's waiting."

"Waiting for what," Brodie said.

"The army is shipping out the Apaches, sending them all to Florida I hear."

"So when they're gone anybody with the map can just waltz right in and take the gold. No Apaches. No ambush. No problem."

"Something like that. Mr. Duphrane, folks say you're the kind of man who knows how to die standing up."

"Oh, my God," said Enid.

Brodie said, "She means I got sand, Enid. That's all."

Cutler placed her half of the map on the bed. "You'll do it, Mr. Duphrane, Brodie?

Enid looked down and shook her head.

Cutler eased the map toward Brodie. "You and Enid, you'll be set up for life."

"Not if he's dead. I don't want you risking it, Brodie," Enid said.

Cutler punched the map gently with her forefinger. "This is your future, Brodie. It's Enid's future, too."

Brodie looked at the map for a long time and then shoved it back across the bed. "Thank you, Ma'am, thank you, but I'm just a rancher."

Enid sighed, relieved.

Cutler took the map. "That's your final say-so?"

"Yes, Ma'am."

"That settles it, then."

"I'm afraid so."

Cutler sat back. "Then, all that treasure is Tule's."

Brodie sat upright instantly. "What did you say?"

"Tule. Tule Henderson. He has the other half."

Brodie leaned forward and gently eased the map from Cutler's hand. Enid sat back, her eyes wide as she stared at the inevitable.

Brodie examined the map. "I'll be leaving tomorrow – partner."

11

A few moments later Brodie stepped on to the porch. Enid followed. Frenchy McCutchen noticed the looks on their faces, he tapped the tobacco from his pipe and, with a nod to Brodie, went inside.

"There's no way I can stop you from going, is there?"

"You know what that man did."

"Brodie, please let it go."

He looked at her as if she was speaking gibberish.

She grasped his arm. "Tule Henderson is a killer and he won't be alone."

"I'll work it out."

"Brodie, no."

"And there's that gold."

"You're going after vengeance...."

"I'll get that too, Enid. Then we'll have something – something more than a cabin on a ranch that's just barely breaking even."

They looked at each other for a long moment. Enid at last sighed. "Aren't you going to kiss me goodbye?"

"Right here?"

Enid wrapped her arms around him and looked up with a sad, hopeful expression. "You come back to me, Brodie Duphrane."

They kissed. When she finally let go, he stepped into the stirrups and mounted his horse. When he was nearly out of town, Frenchy McCutchen stepped back out and joined his daughter by the picket fence.

"He's going after Tule Henderson, isn't he?"

"Yes, Poppa."

"Young Brodie is a good man. He will be back."

"Will he, Poppa? Will he?"

The ranch house was empty when he returned and Hedgeway and Galleta weren't around. He packed up his gear, including several boxes of shells for his Smith and Wesson. He also took a Winchester rifle and a box of shells. Upon leaving, Brodie stopped in the doorway and looked around. He walked back to the table in the kitchen area and wrote out another note. It read:

Tule Henderson.

New Mexico.

He placed a can of beans on the paper, turned and walked out the door.

Brodie rode south and made his first stop among the red-brown buttes, mesas and rock formations in the valley of monuments. He found a good place out of the constant wind near two huge buttes that looked like right and left mittens. He built a fire, made coffee and ate a small meal of bacon and biscuits. Remembering something Hedgeway had told him of the old days when the Indians still ruled the land, he buried the fire, brushed the site with a large tumbleweed so that no footprints or horse prints showed. Anyone looking at the site from a distance would never realize someone had been there. He moved on a mile or so before making camp. He did not make another fire.

Maybe the Navajo are gone; maybe they're not, he thought.

As the shadows cast by a dying sun lengthened his thoughts turned to the task ahead. *The gold is north of Lordsburg. That's where I'll find Tule Henderson – there or thereabouts. Maybe Deming. Maybe Las Cruces, but he'll be around.*

He picked up a stick and made a rough map in the sand. A stab created a small dot in the sand. "Mexican Hat." Far below he drew a waving line running east and west. "The Gila." He pegged several dots following the river line. "Phoenix. Globe City. Safford." Brodie slowly erased the map except for the last dot. He stabbed the stick into the dot. "Lordsburg." He leaned back. *What was it Jess Cutler said? Yeah, tracking him will be easy. Just look for broken women.*

Part Two

12

Brodie kept to himself on the trail south and was soon well into Arizona Territory. He was an excellent shot and the area was rich in rabbit, so he ate well along the way. West of the relatively new town of Tuba City he crossed a section of red, flat rock where he noticed a peculiar set of animal tracks which seemed to be set in stone. They were from some large, three-toed creature that appeared to be carved into the pinkish rock. Each toe had a distinct claw cutting into the mud that had hardened to create the tracks. He shook his head and moved on.

He camped in the rocky flat lands near Flagstaff and bypassed the town, but need for flour and a few other supplies required a stop at Camp Verde further south. His trip into town was brief, lasting no longer than necessary to get the supplies and move on. He stopped by the fort and learned that the Apaches were no longer considered a problem. Most had been rounded up and were waiting up at Holbrook for shipment to Florida. *Cattle to the slaughter*, he thought, but he said nothing about the wisdom of government policy. He was warned about the few renegades thought to be about, but they were considered no more dangerous than the Mexican and American bandits that had moved into the vacuum created by the departing Apaches.

The white rock, almost glowing in the harsh sunlight, the pinion and pine and scrub brush soon gave way to the dominance of tall, green pine and spruce trees dominating the Mogollon Rim. He made a dry camp on the edge of a drop off of several hundred feet. He awakened before dawn and, looking to the east, faced a wall of brilliant orange, as if the sky was afire. The clean smell of green pine was invigorating. He built a small fire to chase off some of the night's chill, made a pot of coffee, and was mounted and riding moments after the sun spiked through the rugged hills below.

He rode across the trail blazed by General Crook more than a decade before. He looked left to the east and then south. He faced forests of towering green trees and rocky canyons either direction.

"Phoenix and the Gila."

Brodie crossed Crook's old path and moved south along a rocky and winding, but well-worn trail. He marveled at how swiftly the land changed, moving from heavy forests to canyons of scattered pine and spruce to broken fields of scrub and grasses. The temperature climbed as he descended. When he came around a bend in the trail he paused. A vast apparently treeless country opened below him. Mountains seemed to pop up from the desert floor like islands in the sea in one of Juan Galleta's tales. Enormous green cacti grew from the land and even the rocks. They were tall with upraised arms like men standing in a hold up. Some were thirty feet tall or more and with nearly half that many arms. The sound of wind blowing through their spines was unlike anything he had heard before – more of a faint, extended hiss. It was a pleasant sound.

"It's an amazement, for sure."

Later and further down the trail he paused again. The wind carried more than the dusky smell of desert sage – a song. A man was singing. He rode on with his right hand near his pistol. The song was sad and in some foreign language. He stopped and looked around. A vast and rugged canyon opened to his left and was so twisted and torn he couldn't see the bottom. A massive pile of weathered, tan-colored boulders blocked his view to the west.

Brodie drew his pistol. "Hello!"

"Hello! Bon ami, hello!"

The voice, clearer now that the man was shouting, came from somewhere in the canyon to Brodie's left. "Who's there?"

"A friend, ami. A friend in need." The voice had a foreign lilt to it, but it was not Mexican or Indian.

"Where the hell are you... friend?"

"Where the hell are you, my new friend? I cannot see you."

"Up here."

"If you are mounted, dismount and walk over to the rock shaped like un crapaud... ah... frog, shaped like a frog."

Brodie dismounted. A large sandstone boulder really did look something like a bullfrog about to leap into the gorge. He cocked his pistol and walked to the edge and looked over. Twenty or so feet down an old man was wedged into the rock face. His arms were outstretched and tied with leather thongs to small rock outcroppings. Brodie holstered his pistol and stared.

"What the hell...."

"If you would be so kind, ami."

Brodie surveyed the scene and picked out the obvious way down to the man trapped between the rocks. He climbed down, being careful to avoid knocking any stones on the old man's head. The thongs were quickly cut and tossed away and, with help, the man was able to scramble out of his trap. "Merci!" Brodie led the way back up to the trail, occasionally pausing to offer a hand.

Back on the trail he offered another hand and within a moment the two were riding Brodie's horse toward the distant communities on the Gila. Brodie said, "I have a few thousand questions for you, mister. First, who are you?"

I am called Montreur – no Jean, no Phillipe, no Charles – just Montreur. And to answer your next question, I was, as you say, waylaid."

"Robbers?"

"Three thieves and not much more wealth after their encounter with me. That, I believe, is why they were so cruel as to imprison me in such a barbarous way. Have you ever seen what the vultures do to a man after the bear or the cougar finishes with him?"

"Can't say that I have."

"Then give thanks to God, for it is not a sight one can forget."

Brodie waited a moment. "So you're broke?"

"No, mon ami. A man who loses money is broke. I have lost more. I have lost my profession."

"What exactly did you lose, old man?"

"Montreur, please. And I lost my... stop!"

Brodie reined in his horse. Montreur slipped off the horse and rushed to the side of the trail. He moved quickly and confidently to a large leather pouch in the dust. He opened it as if it contained crown jewels. "Bonheur!"

"Beg pardon?"

"I am no longer broke." He sniffed inside the pouch. "My spices." He carried the leather bag back. Brodie helped him back on the horse.

"I take it you're some kind of cook, Montreur."

"No, ami. More. I am a chef and these are my... secrets."

"Uh-huh."

"This I will prove to you this evening when we camp."

Montreur was true to his word. Brodie shot another rabbit, which the old man turned into a feast.

"Damnation, Montreur. If you need a job as a cook... I mean chef... my partners and I got a spread up in Utah. We could sure use somebody who knows pepper from gnat dung."

"Perhaps, my friend. But first I have two tasks to accomplish. I must see my old friend *Elias. We trapped together, oh, forty years ago it must be. I would like to see my old friend again. He is a bit crazy I am afraid, but very good company. I hear he is down Tombstone-Bisbee way and he has taken up with a strange woman. I would like to meet the woman who could trap a trapper."

Brodie finished the last of the rabbit and tossed the bones into their small fire. "The other task?"

"I must repay you for saving my life."

"Don't worry about that. You'd have done the same for me."

"I do not worry. But I have a debt and I will see it repaid."

Brodie tossed a few small sticks onto the fire. "I'm not exactly on a business trip, Montreur."

"Your eyes give away more than you think, Brodie. This is a trip of blood, yes?"

"Yes."

"Where will you find this man? Or men?"

"One man, but I doubt he's going to be traveling alone."

"Where will this trail take you?"

"New Mexico, Lordsburg or thereabouts. I'm going to hit the Gila and follow it in."

"Ah, the Gila. I know it well."

Brodie sat up. "You've been there?"

"Many times. It is Apache country."

"Not for long, I hear."

"Perhaps, but it is a dangerous trail. And you have just named how I shall repay my debt. I shall guide you to Lordsburg and then go see my old friend. After that, I perhaps will go see this Utah of yours."

"Montreur, you don't—"

"It is done, Brodie, my friend. Think no more of it."

They enjoyed a smoke without further conversation. As the fire died to embers and the smell of burning mesquite faded, Brodie said, "Montreur, why the hell were you singing back there?"

"When one's life is fading, one might as well sing, eh?"

Brodie grinned, shook his head and rolled over into sleep.

*Elias plays a key role in *Trapp Canyon* by Dan Baldwin.

13

Montreur was up and even had the makings of a small fire going when Brodie awakened.

"Damnation, Montreur, you're a quiet one."

"Silence is a grand ally, my friend, especially when Indians are about. Or bandits."

While Brodie made coffee, Montreur scrounged the forest for edibles and returned with a small armload of vegetation. He mixed it all up with some of his spices and made something of a vegetable stew.

Brodie tasted it with the tip of his tongue and then quickly finished his portion. "I never thought I'd be eating weeds for breakfast. And liking it."

"I have much to teach you then. We have time."

They were back on the trail shortly after sun up. As they came off another mountain trail and the desert opened before them, Brodie stopped. "Would you look at that?"

He pointed across a rolling desert floor to a rugged mountain range to the southeast. A massive peak jutted up above the others – like a Bowie knife into the sky.

Montreur said, "Weaver's Needle, named after my old friend Pauline Weaver. Those are the Superstition Mountains."

"I've never seen any mountains so… intimidating."

"They are an anvil for breaking men."

"And that's where we're going?"

"We will pass close at the western end."

Brodie pointed to a thin line of green their side of the Superstitions. "Is that the Gila?"

"The Rio Salado, Salt River. The Gila is on the far side of the mountains. We can ride toward Mesa City and acquire a horse or, better still, a good mule. I am tired of riding like a Templar."

"What's a Templar?"

"French warrior monks so sworn to poverty that they always rode two men to a horse."

"You Frenchmen come up with some crazy ideas."

"I am not French, my friend. I am Cajun from the bayous of Louisiana."

"All right. Which way?"

Montreur pointed southeast. "I am known at a ranch nearby."

"Is your credit good? You're robbed blind and I'm on short rations as far as money is concerned."

"Ah, they will welcome me with open arms. If they don't shoot me first."

The foreman of the Circle X Ranch welcomed the pair without handshakes or gunplay and Montreur was able to acquire enough credit for a good mule and enough gear and supplies for the long ride to Lordsburg. That gear included a good rifle and an adequate supply of shells. The guests from the north ate well that evening and shared a smoke with some of the ranch hands. They slept well on the floor of the bunkhouse and were up, fed again, and were on their way at sunrise. Montreur insisted that they retrace their route back over the Salt River. He did not say why.

He led the way back north around to the northwestern side of the Superstitions, stopping at a narrow wagon road heading east. He led his horse in a circle and the moved north a hundred yards or so and stopped again. Brodie, who had followed at a distance, caught up. "What is it, Montreur?"

"My mule. The men who took my spices from me came this way." He pointed through the scrub brush. "I recognize the hoof print."

"You want to go after them?"

"No, but we must, my new friend."

"The mule?"

"No. That road back there is new. I suspect it leads to a farm or ranch. The men who took my mule will not be kind to such people." He leaned over, examined the prints in the dirt and led the way back to the road where he turned east to follow. The ruts paralleled the Superstitions until the path was swallowed by foothills when the range turned north.

They saw the narrow stain of gray smoke against the sky before they noticed a lingering smell of bacon. Montreur held up his hand and pointed. Brodie could just make out the shape of an adobe wall in the distance. The old man led him into the brush and eased forward. The main house was a single story adobe structure, a large building with a shaded front porch of wood shaded by a latticework of Ocotillo limbs. A crude wooden barn had been built nearby and both structures were within an oxbow created by a stream, now dry, nearby. A horse and a mule were tied outside the front door, their saddles tossed carelessly on the porch.

"Du mauvais monde. These are bad men." Montreur raised his hand and signaled. The men eased back as the front door of the farmhouse opened. A disheveled woman stumbled out. She was fairly young and attractive. Her hair was unkempt and her dress had been ripped open in the back. A large man followed. He grabbed her by the back of the neck and forced her across the rocky soil to the barn.

"Violer." Montreur spoke under his breath.

"What?"

"An assault."

"No, sir."

Brodie started to move forward, but the Cajun stopped him. "Getting yourself killed will not help that poor woman. Look." He pointed to the door. Another man, clearly not the farmer, stood in the door looking toward the barn. He had a nasty grin on his face. And he was armed. As his partner and the woman entered the barn, the man laughed and went back inside.

Brodie checked the shells in his pistol. "This won't stand."

"I agree, mon ami, but we must act with caution."

"Caution, hell. You know what's going on in there."

"Dead men help no one."

"I can't just let that man—"

"We will do what we are able.

Montreur said, "The man in the barn will be… occupied… I will find it easy to approach and subdue him."

"No."

"You have not heard me out."

"I'll take care of that man in the barn." Brodie's eyes were cold and his voice flat. The old man could see that there was no use in trying to change his partner's mind.

Montreur said, "I will need a signal. Have the woman scream three times."

"Then what?"

"I will approach the ranch avec gout."

"What the hell does that mean?"

"It means you will hear me coming. So will those men."

"Then what?"

"They will see me, recognize me and try to kill me."

"That's not much of a plan, old man."

"It is if you are true to your word. They will be looking at me. And thinking their friend in the barn is doing the same."

"You won't have much time when the shooting starts."

"If you are capable, I will have time enough."

"Let's move. That woman…."

The men eased back into the brush. Montreur moved back up toward the road. Brodie dismounted, hobbled his horse and made his way toward the barn. He crept up, keeping the barn between his position and the house. As he approached the rear door he heard deep laughter and a higher pitched series of grunts. He moved quickly and glanced in. The woman stood her ground holding a three-pronged pitchfork. The side of her face was bloody. She lunged forward with a grunt, but the big man easily dodged the move. He laughed, but the expression was cruel.

She lunged again. He reached out to grab the pitchfork, but she moved quickly and scarred his hand. He reached back, sucked the blood from his hand, and spit at her. He unbuckled his gun belt and placed it over a hook nailed into a support beam. He pulled a large hunting knife from its scabbard. "I ain't going to be gentle on you – like before."

He stepped forward. She lunged again, but he moved to the side quickly and knocked the pitchfork from her hands. She backed away and tripped, falling into the pile of hay in a stall. The big man was so focused on his prey he didn't notice Brodie creeping in through the open back door.

The man jammed the knife into a wooden beam. "First...." The woman scrambled backwards, kicking out with her feet. He easily dodged and was soon on his knees between her legs. "You ain't screaming like before." He wiped his mouth. "Well, we'll—"

Brodie slit the man's throat with his own knife and quickly pulled him away. The woman, still terrified, backed further into the stall. Brodie dragged the man's dying body into another stall. He squatted down and looked into the wide, dying eyes of the other man. "Up in Utah, we call this a 'learning experience.'" The man weakly shook his head, his eyes wide with disbelief. Brodie stood up after the dying breath and returned to the stall with the woman.

She had backed into the corner and retrieved the pitchfork. Brodie threw the knife into a nearby wall and raised both arms. "I'm not one of them, Ma'am." She poked the pitchfork at him, grunting, but the effort was a strain. She trembled.

Brodie kept his distance and squatted down. "Ma'am, I'm here to help you and yours out of this. But you have to help me some."

"Who are you?" She still held the pitchfork.

"My name is Brodie. My partner is out there. His name is Montreur. Tell me about those other men."

She held the pitchfork in trembling hands. "I don't trust you."

"Ma'am, if I was going to hurt you, you'd be hurting pretty bad right now. Are you going to help me save your people or not?"

She dropped the pitchfork, buried her face in her hands and started weeping.

Brodie eased forward and pulled away the pitchfork. "We don't have time for that, now. How many men are left?"

She looked up and wiped her tears on her sleeve. "They hurt me. All of 'em. They been here two days."

"Your family?"

71

"Ben and Melanie, my little girl. They said if I didn't...." She made a feeble attempt to straighten her torn dress. "They said they was gonna make a woman out of her if I didn't... you know. She ain't but ten, Mister."

"They'll pay, Ma'am. Like this one, they'll pay. There are just two left?"

"Three. Hobbs, Peale and one they call Jake."

"There are only three horses out there. Where's the other man?"

"All of 'em inside. Two of 'em, they came in ridin' two on a horse."

"What are they carrying? Weapons."

"Pistols. Two each. Hobbs, he got a shot gun up next to the door."

"Rifles?"

"No." Her eyes were unfocused as if her mind was drifting away.

"Ma'am. I need your help."

"They got Melanie in there."

"Listen! If you want your... if you want Melanie out of there, you have to help me.

"I want you to scream for me. Three times."

She backed away. "Don't touch me."

Brodie held up both hands again. "It's just for show, Ma'am."

"Don't...."

"If you scream three times, we will get Melanie for you. Scream, sharp like you've been cut with a knife."

The woman sucked in a breath and screamed.

"Good. Two more times."

She screamed and screamed again.

Brodie said, "Good. Now you just stay here while we get your little girl." He eased toward the front door of the barn and waited.

14

He did not wait long, for Montreur rode down the path toward the farm singing some Cajun song at the top of his voice. He stopped in the front of the property a few yards west of the house.

"My friends! I have returned! It is I, your old friend Montreur!"

No one returned his call. No one stepped out the door.

"My friends. Are you about!"

The door to the house cracked slowly open, but he could not see who was inside. He dismounted, keeping the mule between himself and the building. Brodie watched closely, his pistol cocked and ready to fire. The large man he had seen earlier stepped outside the door. He held a scattergun and both hammers were pulled back.

"Well, well, well. If it ain't our old Frenchman."

"Hobbs!"

"Come out here. You, too, Peale."

A second man stepped out. He was not as big as Hobbs, but he was every bit as filthy. He held an uncocked pistol in his right hand and a half empty bottle of whiskey in the other. He grinned. "Mon-trower? I'll be damned."

Montreur stepped slowly around the head of his mule. "Yes, mon ami, you are most certainly damned. Va te cacher!"

Hobbs raised the shotgun. "I said git on around here."

Montreur stepped out, drawing his pistol from his belt. He fired his first shot while easing into a crouch. He missed Hobbs by inches. Hobbs jerked aside as the bullet struck the adobe. He fired a single blast, but the shot only scattered dirt and rocks several feet in front of the Cajun. Brodie fired two shots from the barn. One hit Peale in the shoulder; the other shattered the whiskey bottle. Peale twisted, tripped and fell onto the porch. Hobbs turned to face the new danger from the barn just as Montreur fired again. This time the bullet hit the target. The shell ripped through the man's thigh. He turned back toward the old man and fired again. The buckshot missed its target, but shattered the side of the mules head. The animal screamed, stumbled and fell to the ground. Montreur fired two more times. Each shot hit home. The first tore through Hobbs' gut and the second caught him in the throat. Peale scrambled across the rough planks of the porch and raised his pistol. Brodie's final shot blew out half the man's neck. He fell back shuddering a moment and then grew still.

Brodie's face fell when he saw Montreur place his pistol back in his belt. He shouted, "Templars!"

Montreur turned with a puzzled frown. He looked back to Brodie. A look of realization crossed his face. Without hesitation, he dropped to the ground as a shot from the house flew overhead. The Cajun crawled swiftly, clawing his way behind the dying mule as two more shots kicked up the dust within inches of his body.

Brodie aimed, but held his fire. *Melanie and her pop. Can't risk it.*

Nothing happened for a moment and then he heard a muffled scream from the rear of the building.

"Melanie!" screamed the woman. She jumped up and ran across the barn. Brodie grabbed her and held her back.

"Getting yourself killed won't help the little girl."

"He done taken her out back!" Her eyes were wide and wild. "He's gonna do to her what he done to me!"

"No he won't. I promise."

He gently pushed her from the door back into the barn. He looked out and ran to his friend. He squatted low, using as much of the mule as possible as a shield. "Montreur, you all right?"

"Bon. Good. That scream?"

"The other man, he's run off – took a little girl with him."

Montreur looked around. Hobbs and Peale were dead. The woman was stumbling out of the barn, walking in halting steps and with a vacant look in her eyes. Montreur pointed to the house. "Save the girl. I will see to these people."

Brodie stood up and ran into the house. He crouched low and quickly scanned the place, ready to kill if necessary. The back door was ajar. A man was bound to a center post. He had been beaten nearly senseless, but he found the strength to speak. "Melanie… he took my little girl, Mister." His head fell; the effort had caused him to pass out. Brodie cut the ties and dragged him to the nearby bed. The man's eyes opened. "Can you…."

"I'll get your Melanie for you."

"Bless… you."

"And I'll kill the man who took her, too."

Brodie reloaded his pistol and stepped out the back door.

The ground behind the house was covered with tracks, hundreds of them kicked into the rocky soil by the daily activities of a family's daily struggle to live. Outside the small circle of empty ground tall saguaros studded a rocky landscape of tall grasses and scrub brush. Brodie started to dash into the maze, but held back. He stopped, took a deep breath and looked around. He quickly saw two lines of drag marks interrupted by scratches in the dust, breaks in the trail kicked up by a struggling ten year old girl. Brodie followed the tracks.

The girl's struggle made following her movements easy. Small limbs were snapped or bent. Bits of cloth had been ripped by the brush and cactus. He moved swiftly, but cautiously, stalking in a low crouch. Within moments he heard the sounds of struggle. The girl was putting up one hell of a fight from the sound of her muffled screams. He was getting closer. He moved slowly and moved at a faster pace only when the occasional wind rustling through the trees and brush disguised the sound of his footsteps.

Moments later he heard the sound of someone falling and scrambling to get up. He heard a man's scream and then a curse followed by a single gunshot. Brodie rushed forward, ignoring the snapping of dried limbs and leaves beneath his feet. He saw a sandy clearing above a bend in the dry wash that ran back near the house. A broken patch of earth at the edge showed where the pair had fallen. He crouched lower and moved ahead.

A hushed, male voice came from below. "You little bitch. Your time's coming."

"Daddy! Momma!"

"Shut up!"

Brodie heard the wild scrambling of two people on the rocky wash. The girl shouted loudly. The man grunted curses. Brodie stood up and aimed his pistol. The target was short, fat and filthy. His pistol had slipped from its holster and was several feet behind him. His right hand was bleeding, apparently from a savage bite. His face was red with rage; her lips red with the man's blood. He crawled toward the girl. She was on the ground, struggling backwards.

Brodie fired. The bullet struck sand, about two feet in front of the fat man. "Far enough," Brodie said.

The fat man reached for his pistol and came up empty handed. He looked back. He looked up to Brodie. He stared briefly and then smiled. "Amigo."

Brodie shifted his aim to the man, but he spoke to the girl. "Melanie, your momma sent me. Are you all right?"

Melanie stopped scrambling and looked up.

Brodie motioned her up. "Your momma and your pa are all right. Climb on up here with me."

Melanie stood up. She hesitated, looking back and forth between the two men.

"Melanie, your folks are fine, but they need you, girl."

She looked back to the fat man, bent over and picked up as large a rock as she could and threw it at her kidnapper. The man dodged the rock and lunged forward. Brodie fired. This time the shot struck the sand immediately in front of the man.

The fat man backed off and looked up. "Hey, amigo. We can share the pigeon. I don't mind. You go first, amigo."

"Mister, of all the dumb things you could say…." He aimed at the man's back, but hesitated. He looked over to Melanie and then slightly lowered his weapon. *She don't need to see this.* "Melanie, I need you to come up here now. Climb on up like a good girl."

Melanie ran to the side of the wash and used a couple of protruding roots to climb up and out of the wash. She hesitated again, staring at Brodie. "He hurt my momma."

"I know, but he won't hurt anybody ever again. I promise."

She walked to him and grabbed his leg. He spoke without taking his eyes off the fat man in the wash. "Melanie, you can find your way back to your house can't you?"

"Uh-hah. It's right back there." She pointed west.

"Are you sure?"

"Yes, Mister. Me 'n momma, we come back here to pick them cactus fruits. I know the way."

"Go on then. There's a man back there with your folks. He talks funny, but you're all safe with him."

She turned and walked back toward the house.

Brodie stepped over to the edge of the wash and looked at the man below.

Melanie made the journey back to her home easily and quickly. She rushed in the door, but stopped walking when she saw Montreur. He was cleaning up her father's wounds. Her mother rocked quietly in a chair in the corner, her eyes vacant and staring at nothingness. Montreur said, "Come child, your papa is in need of your care." She rushed over, took the wet rag the Cajun offered and began gently wiping her father's forehead. She glanced back at her mother.

Montreur said, "My friend, the man who came for you, is he well?"

"Yes, Mister. He stayed with the fat man."

"Payne," the woman said.

"Are you hurting, Ma'am?"

"The fat man, his name is Payne." A sad and sickly smile formed on her lips and then fell away.

Montreur patted Melanie gently on her head. He walked to the woman and turned her chair so that she faced her husband and her daughter. Her face showed no emotion. "You cannot remain like this for long, Madam. They need you. And you, you need them more."

A gunshot from far behind the cabin startled everyone save the woman. A second shot followed, but only after a moment or so. "My friend, Brodie, he shoots the man who did this."

Another shot sounded.

"He takes his time."

The woman smiled a genuine smile, but remained silent.

They heard three more shots, each separated by at least a moment.

"Mauvais. I do not like this," Montreur said.

15

Brodie and Montreur spent the next two days with Melanie, Ben and the woman; her name was Grace. Ben healed quickly and Melanie, who had not been physically harmed, bounced back even faster. Grace remained in a mild state of shock as she moved through the motions of housekeeping and tending to the needs of her saviors. Her only joy seemed to be the moments spent stroking Melanie's hair before the child fell asleep. Ben was a stern and quiet host, but he took good care of his guests' needs as best he could. He said nothing to Grace and barely looked at her except in stolen glances when she was tending to her chores.

They dragged the body of the unfortunate mule far into the desert. The bodies of the assailants were buried deep in the sand further down from the wash – downwind from the mule. "No flowers for these. Let the smell of death cover their resting place," Montreur said. Their graves were covered with heavy stones, but no stone or even a wooden cross marked their final resting place.

Montreur, enjoying a bite from a twist of tobacco, did make a point of spiting on each grave.

Brodie said, "I guess that's as good a marker as they deserve; better really."

"You took your time with that last one, my friend."

"He earned it."

"I wonder – who were you really killing."

"What do you mean?"

"You told me of your parents. Perhaps you were killing a demon from your past."

"I killed one of the bastards who hurt Grace. He was going to do the same to little Melanie."

"Still, you did not have to take so long. Or make him suffer so much in the killing."

"Men like that can't suffer enough." He turned and walked back to the ranch.

"Mauvais."

They spent their nights in the family's barn, an experience the old Cajun detested.

Late the second night Brodie sat up and looked at Montreur standing by the barn door and looking out. "Why don't you try to get some sleep?"

"She is at it again, my friend."

"Grace?"

"Who else. She sits on that porch and stares into the darkness – her own darkness I fear."

"She ought to be in bed."

"Oui, but Ben will not permit it. I heard them talking this morning, him talking."

Brodie stood up and walked to the door. "What happened wasn't her fault."

"True, but I foresee trouble for this troubled woman."

"Do you think we ought to go over and talk to her?"

"She would not hear." He eased the door shut. "Let us not disturb the poor woman."

"Yeah. She's plenty disturbed already." Brodie's voice betrayed a deep sadness. "It's time we moved on."

When they approached the house for breakfast the next morning Grace was still on the porch. Someone had placed a large canvas bag beside her, but she seemed unaware of the change. Inside, Ben fixed a breakfast of bacon, biscuits and coffee. Afterwards Montreur asked about Grace and the canvas bag.

Ben's voice was without emotion. "It's got her belongins' in it."

Brodie looked stunned. "You can't kick her out of her own house."

"This ain't no whore house."

Montreur said, "The child, Ben, the child."

"She knows. She saw it. We both saw."

Montreur placed his coffee mug on the table, but kept both hands on it. "I have seen worse." He looked up and directly at Ben. "And I have seen stronger men."

"She's a whore. Three times a whore."

Brodie's voice was low and cold. "What the hell did you expect the poor woman to do, Ben?"

"She shoulda' cut her own throat when they was done."

Brodie sat back, a stunned expression on his face. "Are you just going to leave her out there?"

"She ain't none of my concern, nor Melanie's neither." He turned to his daughter and called her over. Melanie came to his side. Her eyes were red from crying, but she said nothing. "Melanie and me, we had a talk this morning."

Brodie's face reddened. "You can't just—"

"I ain't gonna let no whore raise my little girl."

Brodie felt Montreur's hand on his wrist, a gentle, but firm tug.

Ben said, "She's got a sister over in Solomonville. Maybe she'll take her in. That woman ain't spending another night here. We're decent folk in this house." He hugged Melanie. "You men are welcome to stay over as long as you need."

Brodie stood up. His face was flushed and his voice controlled. "I think we have overstayed our welcome." He turned and left.

Montreur sipped the last of his coffee, stood up and walked to the door. "We will take her to Mesa City."

"That ain't goin' to do her no good. Them folks won't have nothing to do with her, not after what I tell 'em. Not when they hear what she done."

Montreur left without saying anything more. A moment later he explained the situation to Brodie.

Brodie said, "It's not like we have a lot of say-so in the situation. But what will we do with her?"

"First, we will take the horses and rigs from those men. We will sell them in Mesa City. Their blood will buy us what we need for our trip to Solomonville."

"Montreur, I have to get to Lordsburg. I can't waste the time."

"Solomonville is on the Gila, my friend, on the way to your destination."

When the three rode away an hour or so later, Grace just stared ahead, silent. Brodie looked back to see Melanie standing on the porch. She started to wave, but Ben grabbed her by the hand, took her inside and closed the door.

16

Brodie remained with Grace on the outskirts of Mesa City while Montreur went into town to sell the horses and gear and pick up enough supplies for the trip downriver to Solomonville. He tried to get the woman to talk, but she refused. Eventually he gave up. Montreur returned a few hours later. He gave half of the money left to Brodie.

"Thanks, but we ought to rat-hole a little for Grace. She'll need something for Solomonville."

"Agreed."

The three moved on south through a desert made farmland by irrigation. Brodie looked back through the fruit trees and cotton plants to the wooden structures of Mesa City. A small community was becoming a town.

"Maybe we should have left her back there."

"I think not. She is a marked woman. Ben will see to that."

"What if there's no sister in Solomonville? What do we do then?"

"Until we know, that is not my concern. First, we must get there."

Fields of domesticated plants quickly gave way to vast fields of saguaro and cholla cactus. Travel was easy and the pathways between the scattered mountains wide and dusty. Toward the end of the day they made camp on the northern banks of the shallow Gila River. Montreur fixed a meal and boiled coffee. Grace ate with them, but said nothing. She did nod when handed a plate, some semblance of awareness.

The Cajun placed a few dried mesquite limbs on their small fire.

Brodie said, "Aren't you worried about Apaches?"

"Nah, boy. They've been rounded up. Besides this is Pima country. They are more likely to share their last bit of food with a stranger than cause trouble."

"I never heard of any Indians like that."

"You have a lot to learn about people, my friend."

Brodie stared into the fire. "The flames, they're something like Grace. They flicker in and out."

"And eventually they die."

Later, Brodie wrapped a blanket around Grace. She sat against a rock, her arms wrapped around her knees. She seemed to nod a thank you. Brodie bedded down on the opposite side of the fire. After the two younger people were asleep, Montreur moved into the desert and found a resting place against a boulder. He had a good view of the camp and of the surrounding desert. He kept watch for some time and then drifted into sleep.

Grace's screaming woke him up just as the sun was breaking over the mountains far to the east. He jumped up and ran toward the camp. The woman was running from the camp. Brodie followed, trying to run and button his britches at the same time.

"Mon dieu." He ran and for an old man, he ran fast and quickly caught up with Brodie. "What have you done?"

"Get her, damn it, before she hurts herself."

They split up, one going east and the other going west. Grace, confused and disoriented, ran back and forth. They soon caught up with her. The woman's eyes were wild with terror as she backed away.

"Don't hurt me again!"

Brodie walked slowly toward her. "Grace, it's us – me and Montreur."

"No!" Her voice was agony and terror.

Brodie stopped and spread his arms. "Grace, we're your friends. Remember?"

He stepped forward slowly. She fell to the ground with another pitiful scream and curled into a fetal position. Brodie stopped and backed away. He looked to Montreur. "I don't rightly know how to handle this, partner."

Montreur thought for a moment and then squatted down. He took a breath and started singing, his voice low and gentle.

Brodie said, "A lullaby?"

Montreur waved him off and kept singing. Slowly Grace's body relaxed and her wild expression faded into a blank stare. The Cajun kept singing, but motioned Brodie in. They lifted her up and walked her back to camp where she curled up in the dirt next to a boulder. Brodie placed a blanket back over her and joined Montreur who was building a small fire.

"What happened, Brodie? What set her off?"

"It's my fault, Montreur. All my fault."

"What did you do?"

"Nothing. I mean... she...."

Montreur poured coffee and water into the coffee pot and placed it on three rocks in the fire placed there for that purpose. He kept his eyes on the fireplace. "Take your time, my friend."

"Hell, Montreur, I stepped out there, way out. I had to use the necessarium."

"Why would—"

"She must have had the same idea and wandered out my way."

"I still do not—"

"She saw my third leg, Montreur. That's what set her off. I didn't even see her until she started that screaming."

"Sweet Jesus."

"What are we going to do?"

Montreur looked over to Grace. She shivered under the blanket. "You had best keep your distance, at least for a while. I shall attend to her needs as best I can."

"Sure. I don't want to go through that again."

"We will eat and break camp. I think it best that you lead for a while."

"But I don't know the way, Montreur."

The Cajun pointed to the Gila. "Follow that."

Grace refused to eat or drink, but before they broke camp Montreur placed a small leather pouch around her neck. "Bacon. When you get hungry, eat."

Brodie led the way as they rode east along the north side of the river toward whatever waited in Solomonville.

17

"It's flowing north." Brodie scratched his head and looked at the shallow, but free-flowing river merging with the Gila.

"The San Pedro. It flows out of the mountains down in Mexico." Montreur cupped his hand and drank from the river. "Sweet. This water's sweet. Toss me the canteens."

Brodie complied and while his partner and guide filled the canteens with water he studied the landscape. Tall cottonwoods provided shade along banks that trailed miles to the south and a luxurious growth of green broke through the rocky brown desert. "A river running north; somehow that just doesn't seem right."

"What is… is, my friend. It will be something to tell your grandchildren about, eh?"

Brodie smiled. "Me with grandkids, me and Enid."

"All the more reason to complete our task. And to be wary doing it."

"How far to Solomonville?"

"Three days easy riding."

The Gila turned northeast from the crossing at the San Pedro. The path was easy to follow, so Brodie led the way and kept his distance from Grace as much as possible. Occasionally Montreur took the lead to get them through troublesome or confusing pathways. At times the way was wide and flat, but at other times canyon walls towered over narrow passageways, but with Montreur's experience and knowledge they made good time. They met a few locals, farmers or ranchers mostly, and exchanged a few words and shared news. Brodie always inquired about Tule Henderson, but no one was familiar with the name or was willing to say so.

They arrived in Solomonville two and a half days later. The town was large and growing. Most of the buildings were of brick or wood, and even the adobe structures were sound and well kept. A mule team of more than twenty animals pulling a wagon loaded with mining equipment passed them at the edge of town. Brodie watched them pass and waited for Montreur and Grace to catch up.

He looked into town. "Where do we start, Montreur. We don't even know Grace's last name."

"And she will not be of much help I am afraid."

Grace stared ahead, her face emotionless and her eyes vacant.

Brodie nodded. "Let's hope we can find that sister. Otherwise I don't know what we're going to do."

The three moved into the busy town. The streets were full of horses, buggies and wagons of all types and people, also of all types, walked along the storefronts. About halfway down the main street Brodie pointed to a sign hanging over the entrance to a modest office. It featured the painted image of a doctor's medical bag with the words

Dr. Sutton
Ring Bell.

Brodie led the way. Grace, riding astride her horse, received a number of disapproving stares from some of the better dressed citizens. They halted in front of the doctor's office and Brodie dismounted. He twisted the knob on the door, ringing the bell inside and a moment later a thin man appeared and opened the door. He was dressed in suit pants, a suit vest, and tie, but was not wearing a coat.

"Yes, Sir. May I help you?"

"Are you this Doc Sutton?"

"Yes. Again, may I help you?"

Brodie pointed back to Grace. Montreur was helping her down from her horse. "We got a sick woman here."

"Bring her in, of course."

Montreur brought Grace in. Brodie stepped back to let them pass and then followed. The Cajun hummed a lullaby as he eased her onto a leather couch. Sutton frowned. A puzzled look followed, as if he was seeing someone from the past he could not quite place. He quickly shook it off and reached for the black bag on his desk. When he reached for it, Brodie raised his arm to block the action. "Doc, we'd better talk first."

"What seems to be the problem, gentlemen?"

Montreur said, "You handle it, youngster. I'll stay with Grace."

Brodie jerked his head toward the front door and walked outside. Sutton followed.

"Doc, long story short – Grace there was hurt bad by three... I won't call them men."

"Three?"

"Yes, Sir. Three men dead now. They took a lot of time with her."

"My God."

"Her old man kicked her out, won't have nothing to do with her anymore."

"What kind of man—"

"I wouldn't call him a man either. Doc, it affected her thinking. Can you take a look at her in that kind of light?"

"Certainly, man."

"We can pay."

"Of course, and thanks for the warning. I'll be easy with her."

"Doc, she's supposed to have a sister here in town, but we don't even know her last name."

"I'm fairly new in town. While I examine the poor woman, why don't you see the town marshal? He's been here since dirt." Sutton pointed down the main street. "Next to the last block. You can't miss it."

"Thanks again. Tell my partner what I'm up to, will you?"

"Certainly."

"Go easy on her, Doc. She doesn't deserve what's happened to her."

"None of them do, Mister, none of them do."

Sutton stepped back into his office and Brodie walked on down the street. He passed a number of saloons, pausing at the first to take in a deep breath. The smell of warm beer and whiskey was an invitation, but he walked on. The buildings were smaller and less impressive as he moved toward the edge of town. Several small buildings were of adobe and one of them was the marshal's office. Brodie crossed the street, knocked on the door and walked inside an office lit only by open shutters. The temperature was relatively cool. The single room housed a desk, several chairs, and other rough-wood office furnishings. There was no jail of iron bars, only a large tree stump in a rear corner. Several large chains ran through holes drilled through the stump. No one was "in jail" at the moment.

Marshal Goodman Torrance was reading the Book of Mormon when Brodie entered his office. He placed the book on his desk and leaned back in his chair. Torrance was an average size man with a clean shaven face that highlighted a bright smile. His eyes were dark and gave the impression of an alert and careful mind. "Can I help you, stranger?"

"I hope so, sir. I surely hope so."

Brodie introduced himself and, in some detail, explained their situation. Torrance's smile faded slowly as the story unfolded. "Let's see what Doc Sutton has to say. Then we'll start looking for that sister of hers."

They walked down the street and entered Sutton's office without knocking. Grace sat on a leather couch, emotionless. Montreur sat beside her, still quietly humming a Cajun lullaby. Torrance looked at Grace and then quickly to Sutton.

"I'll be damned." Torrance caught himself. "Pardon, Ma'am."

Brodie said, "Like I said, Grace doesn't say much."

Sutton cleared his throat. "They say she has a sister hereabouts. Do you—"

Torrance said, "Yeah."

Montreur stopped humming. Brodie stepped forward. "You know her sister?"

"Yes, Sir. I do."

"That, mister, is a relief."

"Maybe. You'd best come with me."

"Where, Marshal?

"Big Minnie's Rose Petal."

"Who is Big Minnie?"

"She's your friend's sister."

"Where can we find her?"

"That's easy, son. Big Minnie runs the biggest whorehouse this side of Phoenix."

18

Big Minnie's Rose Petal was an imposing brick building at the far end of town and one block over from the main street. It was two stories tall and featured a shaded porch around the front two thirds of the building and looked more like a fancy residence than a place of business.

Torrance said, "Before the town got civilized, Minnie used to parade her girls out there in the open. I had to shut that down."

"But not the brothel."

"Hell no. That's one of the most profitable businesses in this part of the country. Minnie is a skinflint, but she pays her taxes on time. And she keeps her girls clean."

"That doesn't matter to me."

"I was just letting you know."

"Marshal Torrance, I just want to see Grace left in good hands and to move on. I have business in Lordsburg."

"Well, sir, Minnie's hands are capable. I don't know if you'd call 'em *good* or not."

They stepped up on to the porch, Torrance in the lead. He knocked on the door. A small, well-dressed Negro opened the door. "Marshal Torrance, Sir. How good to see you again. Please come in, Sir."

Big Minnie's parlor lived up to the Rose Petal name. It was well-appointed with red, pink and white as the dominant colors. Images of roses decorated the carpet, wallpaper, framed paintings, vases and just about everything that could hold a design. Brodie removed his hat and held it before him in both hands.

The Negro said, "Something to drink, Sir?"

"Not today, Clairville. We need to see Minnie."

Clairville looked to Brodie. "Perhaps something for you, Sir?"

"No, thanks."

Clairville bowed slightly. "I will inform madam that you are here. I am certain she will be down directly."

Torrance said, "As if she don't already know I'm here. On second thought, pour me a shot of that good whiskey."

"Certainly."

Clairville stepped over to a large, intricately carved wooden cabinet, which held several bottles of excellent liquors. He poured a shot, paused and doubled it, and brought it to the marshal.

Torrance accepted it and the Negro turned and left the room. "Don't let Clairville fool you, Mr. Duphrane. He plays the piano and sometimes the fool, but he's Minnie's bookkeeper and the real secret of her fortune, which is substantial I might add."

"This Big Minnie, she knows Grace's sister?"

Heavy footsteps indicated someone coming down the stairs. Torrance said, "See for yourself."

Big Minnie entered the room smiling. "Marshal Torrance, business or pleasure?"

Brodie's jaw dropped. Big Minnie was an oversize version of Grace – the same facial structure, the same hair, the same eyes, and even the same slight cleft in the chin. "I'll be damned."

Minnie laughed. "Perhaps, young sir. We aim to please."

Torrance killed his whiskey. "Minnie, Mr. Duphrane has something to discuss with you."

"You done got serious all of a sudden, Goodman."

"It's something of a serious matter, Minnie." He looked to Brodie.

"Your sister, Grace, Miss Minnie. We brought—"

Minnie's smile disappeared and was replaced with a snarl. "Miss High 'n Mighty? What's she got to do with me? And who the hell are you?"

Brodie took half a step forward. "I'm just someone passing through. Grace, she's had a bad time."

"Well, ain't that just too bad." Minnie stalked over to the liquor cabinet and poured herself a drink. "She's here? With you?"

"Yes, Ma'am. Me and a friend of mine."

"Well, the three of you can just keep on going."

"We can't take her where we're going, Ma'am."

Torrance said, "She's your sister for Chrissakes, Minnie. Anybody can see that."

"I ain't got no sister... least of all some holier than thou Bible thumper."

"She's been hurt, Ma'am. Her thinking isn't right either."

"Her thinking ain't never been right, young sir." Minnie poured another drink and immediately killed it. "I got nothing to do with *the princess.*

Brodie looked helplessly to Torrance. The marshal walked to Minnie and accepted another drink. "Minnie, your own flesh and blood...."

"Blood don't mean family."

"She's your sister, Minnie. You owe it—"

"I don't owe Miss Hifalutin squat!"

"She's in a bad way, Ma'am," Brodie said.

Torrance took the glass from her hand and gently placed it on the cabinet. "Minnie, would you at least come look at the poor woman?"

Minnie's upper lip curled. "All right. I'll go look at the bitch. I could use a good laugh."

Minnie excused herself to go change clothes. Clairville returned, sat down at the piano and began playing a soft tune. "Miss Minnie will be back directly, gentlemen. In the meantime, is there some service I could perform for you?"

Torrance laughed. "Quit that plinking, Clairville. I know you're Minnie's eyes and ears. Mr. Duphrane and I won't be whispering any secrets for you to steal."

Clairville lowered the volume of his playing, but continued.

Brodie sat down and put his hat back on. "Clairville, why is Miss Minnie so all-fired hateful to her sister? Do you know?"

"No, Sir. She has rarely spoken of the woman and when she has the comments have been unpleasant."

"Do you have any idea why?"

Clairville glanced around and spoke in a low voice. "Faith, that's her real name you know, some time ago Faith got herself... ah, wearing the bustle on the wrong side as they say."

Torrance nodded. Brodie looked puzzled. "I don't understand."

Torrance said, "She got baby bound."

Clairville said, "Without benefit of marriage. Apparently, her family, this Grace of yours in particular, was not supportive. I believe that is what led her to become an erring sister."

"A common tale," Torrance said.

"I sense considerable bitterness there, Marshal."

Torrance turned to Brodie. "You might have a bigger problem on your hands than you thought, Mr. Duphrane."

Minnie's heavy steps on the stairs announced her arrival before she entered the parlor. Brodie stood up and removed his hat again. Minnie wore a bright red dress decorated with large black and red rose patterns. Her hat, also black and red, was equally garish. She carried a parasol and it, too, was red and black.

Torrance said, "Always making a statement, eh, Minnie?"

"I call it advertising." She turned to the piano player. "Clairville, grab your coat. I want your opinion on this situation. On this… woman."

"Yes, Ma'am."

Outside, Minnie offered her arm to Torrance. "Goodman, if you please."

"Minnie, you know I can't do that. Not in public."

"Hmmf!" She stopped walking and let Brodie catch up. She held out her arm. "Mr. Duphrane?"

Brodie took her arm and they walked down the street.

Brodie blushed the entire way.

19

"This... thing is my sister?"

Brodie sat beside Grace. "What's left of her."

"She's had a bad time of it," Montreur said.

Minnie turned her face to the Cajun. "I know you. Frenchy, right?"

"Cajun. And, yes, I have been to your establishment before."

"I never forget a... face." Minnie smiled. "You always was well-heeled for a Frenchy, or Cajun or whatever you call yourself. What say we—"

Torrance cleared his throat. "You want to take care of this business first?"

"She ain't no business of mine."

"She's your kin," Brodie said.

"Take her to a snake pit."

"What!" Brodie jumped to his feet.

Torrance stepped forward. "She means asylum, Mr. Duphrane, a place for people who ain't well in the head."

"I know what it means." He turned to Minnie. "You can't do that to her."

Minnie walked over to her sister and sat down. She slapped her gently on her cheeks. "Sis, you in there, sis?" Grace stared straight ahead. Minnie stood up and walked around the woman, giving her a good once-over. "My, my, my. How the mighty have tumbled." She walked to the door. "Clairville, step outside and let's you an' me make some chin music."

"Yes, Ma'am."

Clairville opened the door and followed her outside where they discussed the matter for several moments. When they returned, Minnie walked directly to Brodie. "How much?"

"Ma'am?"

"What do I owe you for her?"

"Nothing, Ma'am. We were just trying to bring her home."

Torrance said, "Minnie is just trying to repay you for your efforts. That's all."

"It was no effort at all, was it, Montreur?"

The Cajun just shook his head and then looked to the floor. "It is time for us to leave, my friend." He stood up and walked out of the room.

Minnie said, "I'll take her off your hands. But she's gonna have t' earn her keep. I ain't running no charity."

Torrance said, "What do you have in mind, Minnie?"

"This ain't none of your business, Goodman."

Torrance walked to his desk and sat down. Minnie nodded to Clairville and the two walked over to Grace and lifted her up. "Get the damn door will you, Duphrane."

Brodie jumped up and followed the command. Minnie and Clairville guided Grace through the door and into the street. Brodie watched them lead her away and then shut the door. "I want to thank you, Marshal, for all your help."

"Such as it was. Are you all right with this?"

"Yes, Sir. We got Grace to her family. Now I can go on about my business."

"What would that business be, Mr. Duphrane?"

"Tule Henderson."

Torrance looked at Brodie for a moment. "I take it you're headed Lordsburg way."

"That's his country these days. Or so I hear."

"You hear right. Watch your back over there." Torrance stood up. "I need another drink. He walked to the door and escorted Brodie out. Montreur stood nearby. "You men are welcome to stay as long as you want. But if I was you, Mr. Duphrane, I'd be getting on with that business of yours." He was looking down the street. Minnie and Clairville were turning down the street toward the whore house.

20

Torrance turned and watched Brodie and Montreur leave in the opposite direction, watched until they disappeared into the landscape. He went back in his office, made coffee and took care of paperwork. Later, he walked down to the telegraph office where he collected a few messages and sent one of his own. He moved on to the town's largest mercantile store where he picked up a handful of his favorite cigars – Cubans. They were expensive for the proprietor, free for law enforcement. Torrance made his afternoon round and stopped off at his home where he told his wife he would be home late that evening.

He returned to the office and killed time with meaningless chores until the sun was sinking low. When he left he paused to look at the wanted posters pinned to a board near the door. His eyes focused on the poster featuring Tule Henderson.

He spoke softly, almost a whisper. "Good luck to you, Mr. Duphrane. You are going to need it." Torrance stepped out, locked the door and walked down the street and turned toward Big Minnie's place.

Brodie and Montreur continued moving north toward the band of green marking the Gila River. The Cajun was unusually insistent upon putting some distance between them and the town. He had even refused to consider Brodie's suggestion of a brief respite in one of the local saloons. "I bought a bottle. We can drink on the way," Montreur said.

They rode in silence for a considerable amount of time before Montreur reached into one of his bags and retrieved a bottle of rye. He uncorked it and drank before offering the bottle to Brodie.

"Later, but thanks," Brodie said.

"Drink now. You will need the effect later."

"What are you getting at? What effect?"

"Realization, my young friend. Drink."

"Whatever you say." He accepted the bottle. They passed it back and forth several times before reaching the Gila. Brodie reined in his horse. "Oh, no."

"Ah."

Brodie turned his horse so that he faced south, toward Solomonville.

Montreur turned also. Each man looked back toward the small community now lost in the distance. "We can return, Brodie, and you can try to undo what we have done. Or we can continue your journey to Lordsburg. It must be one or the other."

"My God."

Montreur handed over the now half-empty bottle of whiskey. "Drink well. I have another, my young friend."

"We're going to need it." Brodie turned and moved back toward the Gila. Montreur followed. He glanced back once, accepted the bottle from Brodie, and rode on.

Goodman Torrance walked down the wooden sidewalk. The setting sun gave the dusty streets a golden glow, a beauty marred by the smell of horse and animal manure. He turned at the end of the street and walked to Big Minnie's Rose Petal where he climbed the steps and knocked on the door.

Minnie met him. "I figured I'd be seeing you tonight."

"Where's your usual doorman?"

"Clairville has some bookkeepin' to fiddle with. Come on in this house."

Minnie led him to the parlor. He nodded or said hello to the women who weren't already playing hostess. She poured him a double shot of good whiskey. "I done paid up on my taxes and fines. Doc Sutton checked out my girls this week. We ain't got no drunks causing a ruckus. So, you ain't here on city business are you" She smiled broadly.

Torrance returned the smile. "I thought I'd be first to meet the new girl."

"She's in the Pink Room."

"I know the way."

Torrance finished his drink and glanced upstairs.

As he turned, Minnie grinned broadly and said, "She's real quiet like, but she'll do anything you want, Goodman. Anything at all."

Behind the parlor, in the business office, Clairville worked on his books. He opened a ledger, dipped the nib of his pen in a bottle of ink and added a name to the list of prostitutes working in Big Minnie's Rose Petal.

The Princess.

Part Three

21

Montreur led the way east along the southern side of the Gila. He followed animal runs that few men other than the Indians could follow. The growth was thick and became more of a challenge as they moved along the banks. While stopping to drink from the gently flowing waters they were surprised by four javalina. Montreur drew his pistol, but the beasts rushed by and disappeared into the underbrush as swiftly as they had appeared.

"Nasty animals, dangerous, too," Brodie said.

"Good eating though… if you are hungry enough."

"Maybe. If you use enough of those spices you carry around."

At one of the many bends in the river, Montreur halted and scanned the path behind them. He cocked his head, listening. He even sniffed the air.

"What do you see," Brodie said.

"Just what I want to see."

"And what's that?"

"Nothing.

"Why are you looking for nothing, Montreur?"

"This man you are hunting, Tule Henderson. This is his country, right?"

"That's what I hear."

"A man like that has few if any friends, but he will have many eyes and ears about."

Brodie stood up in his stirrups and looked back. "You think we were followed?"

"No. But I think now is a good time to leave the river. We can cut south and take a far easier road toward Lordsburg."

Montreur moved southeast away from the river into a rough country of low, rugged mountains, desert washes, open plains studied with cactus and patches of dry grass. Soon the river disappeared below the horizon as if it no longer existed.

Brodie said, "How soon until we get to Lordsburg?"

"Not soon enough for you, my friend. Too soon for me."

"What the hell do you mean by that?"

"I feel some responsibility for your life. Je reste a vous redevoir. A debt I must repay."

"You don't owe me any debt."

"I fear this man may know you are coming. We need information."

"How would Henderson know we're… I'm coming for him?"

"You talk too much." Montreur spurred his mule gently and rode away. Brodie followed and soon caught up.

Two days later Brodie spotted a line of green in the distance. "The Gila?"

"Oui. We rest for a day shortly."

"Lordsburg?"

"No, my friend. Duncan. We are a day or so from your destination. Information is more important sometimes than the bullets in your pistol. I know someone here who may help."

"Who would that be?"

Montreur laughed loudly. "The king, my friend, the King of New Mexico."

They reconnected with the Gila when they descended from the plateau into Duncan. The small community was busy. A narrow gauge railway ran through the town, connecting the growing population with multiple opportunities provided by the copper mines just to the north. A wide swath of newly cultivated fields represented the growing agricultural face of the town. Most of the activity was south of the river. The northern banks were virtually deserted, although the foundations of a few buildings and even an intact or moderately intact structure still resisted the erosion and neglect claiming the others.

Montreur stopped and dismounted in front of Tejander's Café. He tied off his horse and entered the building. Brodie followed. Inside,

Montreur moved to a table in the rear and sat down facing the door and with his back to the wall. Brodie joined him as a waiter approached.

Montreur said, "Your coffee, boy. How is it?"

The young man grinned. "Well, mister, you set a spoon in it upright and it'll stay that way 'til sundown."

"Good! Two cups and quickly, my friend."

"Would you men care for a look at our menu?"

"Steak, potatoes and biscuits."

"Make it two," Brodie said.

"Yes, Sir. I'll get that coffee right away."

The coffee was hot, the food good, and the portions generous. They ate well and finished off the meal with apple pie. When the waiter came to buss the table, Montreur said, "Where might my friend and I find your king?"

"That old coot ain't no king."

"Nonetheless, where would he be holding court today?"

"Court? Oh, uh, you men'll probably find him at what he calls the royal gardens. That'd be the big ol' cottonwood just west of town. Look for the fishing pole. Likely, he'll be at one end or the other."

Within moments the two men crossed the rough bridge over the Gila and rode easily along the northern bank. Montreur waved his arm at the waste. "This used to be Purdy, but after the railroad came in they changed the name to butter the backside of some... somebody."

"This king of yours, he can help me find Henderson?"

"He is old, like me, and like me he is a man of the mountains. He ranges far and wide. If there is news of this Henderson, he will have it.

The mayor was not beneath the cottonwood, so they turned and headed back to the ruins of Purdy. A portion of one adobe building stood taller than the rest. Only three crumbling walls remained, leaving a wide door of sorts facing the river. A mixed-breed cat watched them intently from atop one of the walls. It jumped down and raced away as they approached.

Montreur spoke softly, "As you may have ascertained, my old friend appears to be somewhat weak above his ears."

"Crazy you mean."

"It is an act – I think – that has served him well. He hears much and forgets nothing."

"Does he really think he's a king?"

"It is only important that he think we believe he is a king."

"If it gets me to Henderson, I'll play along."

Montreur shouted, "Your majesty!"

A strong voice revealing some age responded from the far side of the ruin. "Who approaches the castle?"

"Montreur, you old son of a bitch. And a friend."

An old man stepped out from behind the building. He was rail thin, long of hair and wearing a tattered business suit. He was buttoning up his britches as he approached. "Excuse me, gents. The king was on his, uh, throne."

Montreur dismounted and hugged the old man. "How are you, my old friend?"

"Majestic as always."

Montreur turned to Brodie. "Step down and meet Jasper Clegg, King of all New Mexico."

Brodie dismounted and approached the two men. "Proud to meet you, King."

Clegg looked him over. "Your squire, Sir Montreur?"

"Something like that, your majesty."

"Well, come on in to the castle and have a sit down."

Clegg led them inside the ruin where he sat down on a three-legged stool. Brodie and Montreur each sat on a bench against the walls. The interior was sparse, but neat and clean considering its exposure to the elements. Clegg noticed Brodie looking around. "It gets a bit dicey when it rains, young squire, but I have a canopy." He pointed to a rolled up canvas tarp in the corner.

"We could use your help, my friend," Montreur said.

"Ah, you seek a boon."

"I'm seeking a man," Brodie said.

Clegg looked to Montreur. "Your squire needs training in manners."

"Clegg, my friend, your majesty, my… squire is seeking a villain, a most dangerous and evil foe.

"A quest!"

"Exactly." Clegg reached behind his chair into a wooden box and pulled out a battered bowler with a tattered brim and ceremoniously placed it on his head. He reached in again and pulled out a thick wooden walking stick which had numerous symbols carved into it. He hefted it and stamped it three times on the hard dirt floor. "State your request."

Brodie leaned forward, but before he could speak Montreur held up his hand. Brodie leaned back as Montreur spoke. "My friend here is looking for a man called Tule Henderson."

"A miscreant. And a most foul and dangerous man."

"Can you help us track him down?"

"Your squire's quest, is it in a noble cause?"

"Damn it, Clegg. He killed this young man's mother. And others."

Clegg leaned back against the wall and tipped his hat back up on his head. He poked the staff into the ground several times. He leaned forward and spoke without the kingly tone of voice. "Henderson is in Lordsburg."

"We know that," Brodie said.

"Word is he's waiting on something to happen before making his next move."

Brodie said, "The Apaches, once they're shipped of he's got a plan."

"I have been hearing a different word."

Montreur said, "What word would that be, my friend?"

"I hear he's waiting on somebody, somebody coming to kill him. I take it, now, that Henderson is waiting on your young friend."

22

"That can't be." Brodie half stood up before Montreur pulled on his arm. He sat back down.

Montreur said, "What do you know, my friend?"

"My kingdom is wide and I see and hear many things, many things. When you are crazy people aren't so careful about what they say. This man Henderson has been making purchases for several months, slowly so as not to draw attention. But nothing escapes the eye of the King."

"Mining equipment," Brodie said.

"I think so… picks, shovels, a wagon and a load of wood to go in the wagon. He takes his time and buys only a little now and then."

"You say he's waiting for Brodie?"

"I said he is waiting for someone. Now, only we three know who."

Brodie said, "How?"

Montreur said, "You talk too much."

Clegg jammed the walking stick hard into the ground. "Precisely. In recent weeks I have heard bits and pieces of talk. Word is that someone is coming for Henderson. He knows and he waits."

Brodie leaned even further forward. "But he doesn't know who?"

"Only that someone is coming."

Montreur said, "Malchance. This is bad luck. Where is he? Do you know?"

"He and a few men are holed up in an old adobe at the edge of Lordsburg. The townsfolk say he pretty much keeps to himself, except when he's drunk. They don't like him, but that ain't going to help you boys out none."

Brodie said, "What about the sheriff? The marshal?"

"Buffaloed. They won't risk a good paying job to help strangers."

Montreur looked to Brodie. "Do you wish to continue your... quest?"

"You have to ask?"

"Then it's just you and me, my friend."

Clegg stood up and held out his staff. He cleared his throat and his guests immediately followed. "You forget, gentlemen. The King of New Mexico as deigned to grant your boon." Clegg stood perfectly still with his eyes gazing into the distance.

No one said anything else for a moment. Clegg continued to stare. Brodie looked to Montreur. "Are we supposed to bow or something?"

"God only knows. Let us for now depart."

Montreur offered a slight bow and backed out.

"What the hell." Brodie bowed and backed out, too.

As they were about to mount their horses, Clegg stepped to the edge of the ruin and nodded for Montreur to join him. Montreur obliged. Clegg spoke softly and in a normal voice. "It's about time for the King to visit his subjects. I'll ride over to Lordsburg for a little look-see tomorrow."

"Thanks, Clegg."

"Hell, it's getting to damn peaceful around here. I could use a little excitement. You boys best stay out of town – too many eyes and ears. Camp out up river a bit and stay low. I'll find you in a couple of days."

"Thanks again, old friend."

Montreur started to turn when Clegg held out his hand, palm up.

"I am not going to kiss your ring, Clegg, king or no king."

"I was thinking more along the lines of getting a dollar from you. I sure could use a bottle tonight. It gets cold here in Camelot when the sun goes down." He winked.

Brodie and Montreur rode downriver until Duncan was out of sight. They watered the horses well, refilled their canteens and rode about a mile to the northeast toward some low hills. They made camp between two hills. Their small campfire was visible only from one direction and it was dowsed after they had prepared a meal. By sundown the camp was dark.

"We have been seen by enough people," Montreur said.

Brodie broke in half a stick he had been fiddling with. The snap was like the crack of a small caliber pistol. "Damn it, I ought to be riding into Lordsburg."

"You would be riding to your death."

"Henderson doesn't know me."

"He knows someone is coming. He will be watching everyone." Montreur paused. "Like that snake at your feet."

Brodie saw the long, black shape near his boot and scrambled back.

Montreur laughed and threw a pebble. It bounced off the stick that had so frightened his young partner.

Brodie eased back to his previous position. "Damn you."

"I was making a point, my young friend. You see a stick and think it a snake. You see a sheriff and you think him a man of the law. You see a woman and you think her virtuous."

"What the hell is your point?"

"You are not ready to enter Lordsburg. Let Clegg be your eyes and ears for the moment."

"I hate just sitting on my ass."

"But that, my friend, is the best place to sit."

The conversation rambled on for a while. Montreur was first to roll over and go to sleep. Brodie stared up at the stars, breathed in the desert aroma of sagebrush and listened to the rippling flow of the distant Gila. He snapped half a dozen more twigs before closing his eyes and drifting away to sleep.

23

The next two days were a hell of nothingness for Brodie. At sundown of the second day he sat atop a rocky outcrop that provided a view of the plain and the river. He tossed small pebbles into the sand and continually looked east, toward Lordsburg. Montreur joined him.

"You are, as they say, chomping at the bit to get yourself killed," Montreur said.

"I just want to get this thing done."

"You call killing a man a *thing*?"

"He's not a man, nor any with him."

"As you have told me, you have just cause. But a cause can carry a man too far. You must control your heart."

"I intend on killing Tule Henderson. He earned what's coming to him. But there's more to it than that."

"He has done you another wrong?"

"Not me. A woman back in Mexican Hat. He hurt her pretty bad, but that's not... she gave me part of a map. A gold mine north of Lordsburg."

"Mon Dieu! That explains much of your passion."

"It's not the gold. It's what that gold will do – after I kill Tule Henderson."

"You suffer from two fevers."

"I mean, I plan on marrying. Enid is her name. That gold will give us a good start. Better than most."

"A wife. This is good. This is what you need."

"I'm not a greedy man, Montreur. You're in for half of whatever's out there."

Montreur joined in the pebble tossing. "I would not know what to do with wealth."

"I figure you'll work out something."

"If there truly is a mine. If there is gold in the mine. And if we live to find it."

"I'll admit, that's a lot of *ifs.*"

"Such is life."

"One of my partners says *if* is the center of *life.*"

"That is a very silly thing to say."

"You have to know Juan."

Brodie stood up, hefted a larger stone and threw it into the lengthening shadows.

Montreur said, "Let us visit a saloon before you explode."

"We ain't left yet!"

An hour later the two outsiders were inside Cheney's #1 Saloon, a long and narrow building with a large, polished wood bar on the right and several small tables for gaming on the left. The smell of good cigars and whiskey mixed with the clatter of the billiard table in the back and the loud banter of men blowing off steam from another hard day. Two men playing guitars provided lively music from a corner near the billiard table. No one, other than the bartender, paid them any mind as they stepped up to the bar.

"Whiskey. Beer chaser," Montreur said.

"The same," Brodie said.

Montreur killed his whiskey and turned, back to the bar, to observe the activities in the saloon. Brodie killed his drink in two swallows and then rolled the small glass against the top of the bar with his fingers.

Montreur glanced over. "A wise hunter keeps his eyes on the prey about him."

"What?"

"Do not turn away from so many men with guns, Brodie. It is a bad policy."

Brodie stopped fiddling with the shot glass and turned around. "Do you think somebody here knows who I am? Why I'm here?"

"Everyone here knows we are strangers. One or more will surely know the man you are seeking."

"I have gone and messed up, haven't I?"

"No, my friend, but the element of surprise you are counting on is a pipe dream. Nonetheless, if we are wise, you will have your revenge, your prize, and that young woman of yours."

"Enid. That's her name."

Montreur twisted back toward the bar. "Two more whiskeys."

When the drinks arrived Montreur said, "To the woman who waits."

"To Enid."

A middle-aged woman who had been working her way through the bar finally made her way to the two strangers. She was attractive, but aging quickly.

"Did I hear the word *Enid*? That's my name, too."

"Of course," Montreur said. He winked at the woman.

She winked back and eased close to the old man. Montreur said, "That is too bad. I am looking for a Marie."

She moved even closer. "Marie is my middle name."

"Faire la connaissance. It is a pleasure to meet you, Enid Marie."

"Oh, a Frenchman all the way out here."

"Oui, madam. Cajun French."

"I been to New Orleans once."

Brodie rolled his eyes and looked away. The door at the rear of the saloon slammed open. A large man, filthy from a day working at the rail yard, stomped in the room. He looked around and didn't appear to see what he wanted. He stepped forward. Several men moved out of his way as he passed the billiard table. The man stopped when he could see the front of the bar. He shouted, "Carlene! Get away from that sum-bitch!" He stepped forward with clenched fists.

Montreur looked to Enid Marie. "You would be Carlene, eh?"

"You'd better skedaddle, mister."

She backed away as the big man approached. He stared at Montreur, ignored Brodie and turned to the prostitute. He grabbed her by her arm and twisted. She shrieked in pain. He slapped her across her face – brutally. The locals nearby backed off. The man raised his hand again. Carlene cringed and braced herself for the blow.

"No, Pink! Don't—"

Brodie smashed his beer mug into Pink's face so fast and with such power that the thick glass cracked. As Pink staggered back Brodie kicked him in the groin and the big man doubled over. Brodie brought the mug down on the back of the man's skull and this time the glass broke into pieces. Pink fell to the floor and hit his head on a spittoon. He slipped further and the foul sludge dumped on his face. Brodie, his face red and his eyes wide, raised the remainder of the mug up and threw it on the man's limp body.

Montreur grabbed his friend and pulled him back. "Enough!"

"I'll kill him!"

"Brodie!" Montreur pulled him further back, the old man showing surprising strength. "Get that man out of here! Rapide! Quickly!"

Three men who had backed off earlier moved in and started dragging the unconscious man away.

The bartender said, "Tie him to the old tree out back and let him sleep it off. Tie him good and tight."

Brodie settled down as the man was pulled away and Montreur released his hold. "Avoir du curage. You have guts, my friend. But you are an imbecile."

Brodie shook off his anger, breathing deeply and looking at the men gathering around him.

Montreur leaned over the bar. "My friend, he has cause for such behavior."

"Hell, mister, don't nobody here give a damn. Pink's been asking for trouble – just a matter of time until somebody climbed up 'n down his backbone."

Brodie leaned against the bar, his eyes still on the men watching him. He breathed heavily. "I guess we ought to call the law."

"Hell, mister, the only law in Duncan is the last man standing. I recon it's your call and I bet I already know the verdict."

Montreur said, "I suspect it is time we made our leaving."

"Hell, no, mister. You're friend here done whupped up on Pink Garnett. That calls for a round on the house."

The matter seemed to be settled. The Duncan men eased back to their tables. One of them even patted Brodie on the shoulder. The bartender poured two more beers and two more shots of whiskey. "Like I said, on the house."

"Merci bien."

"What he said." Brodie killed the whiskey in one swallow and started in on his beer. "No trouble, then?"

"Naw. Pink's dumber than a bucket of bolts, but he learns quick like. You won't see much of him while you're here. You boys in town for long?"

Brodie looked down. Some of Pink Garnett's blood stained the side of his boot. He tried to scrape it off on the brass rail. He looked back to the bartender. "Depends."

The bartender poured another shot. "Depends on what, if you don't mind the inquiry?"

"Depends on if Tule Henderson walks through that door."

"Brodie...." Montreur slightly shook his head.

The bartender said, "My name's Harper. And if you're going after Tule Henderson I'd like to shake your hand."

They shook hands and Harper said, "I might be the last man to do that with you. Tule, he's trouble, real trouble. But I guess you know that."

"He has had some experience with the man." Montreur said.

"Ain't we all." Harper looked to the back of the bar and shouted. "Murillo, get your ass down here."

A young Mexican rushed over. "Si, Senor Harper."

"Go back into the storeroom and bring me a bottle of good whiskey, the one with old Ben Franklin on the label. We got to celebrate. This here fellah is gunning for Tule Henderson. You hear that, he's gunning for Tule."

"Si." The young man looked over Brodie. "Bueno suerte, mister."

"Hurry up, Murillo." Harper turned back to Brodie. "Might be the last good whiskey you get, too. But like the kid said, good luck, sir."

Montreur urged Brodie to move on, but the young man was still full of rage and doing his best to calm down. Harper supplied a few more drinks after the bottle of the good stuff arrived. He refused to accept payment for the next two rounds. Brodie purchased a third. Harper kept the conversation going with a series of questions and eventually Brodie's rage subsided.

Montreur finished his beer and placed it on the bar with emphasis. Brodie ignored the implied message and continued sipping his own drink. Montreur said, "Where's the necessarium these days, Harper?"

"Out back. You can't miss it. Kick Pink when you walk by."

Brodie killed his beer. "I'll wait for you out by the horses." He turned and walked toward the front door, almost stumbling over the broken beer mug at his feet.

Montreur nodded and walked to the rear of the bar. He stepped outside. If he had not received directions to the privy, the heavy smell would have provided a road map. He walked around the tree where Pink Garnett was tied. The man was still out cold. Montreur walked on and stopped at the door of the privy. He put his hand on the wooden latch and paused. "Miche en flute!" He snorted and walked around the privy and stepped into the shadows of steps leading up to the second floor of the building next door. He unbuttoned his pants and urinated into the dust, carefully avoiding soiling the building. When finished he walked to the side of the saloon and made for the street.

A powerful gunshot blasted the nighttime quiet. Three more shots followed in rapid succession, followed by a pause and one more shot. He ran to the street. Two men on horses rode out of town as fast as their mounts could take them. By the time he made it to the front of the saloon several men had gathered about a man lying in the dark street. He pushed his way through.

Harper stepped up and said, "It's your friend. He's been killed."

The Duncan men stood back from Brodie as Montreur rushed over, bent down and examined his friend.

Someone said, "We got a doc, mister, but he's out helpin' birth a baby south of town."

"Please, back away," Montreur said. He bent over closer to look at Brodie's wounds. The men backed off a few paces. Montreur took off his hat and held it across his chest. He placed his hand on Brodie's head. Harper shook his head and Murillo, standing next to him, crossed himself.

Harper said, "We can't just leave him in the streets like that."

Montreur looked up. "Is there, perhaps, a wagon I could borrow?"

Someone in the back of the small gathering said, "Sure, mister. You can borrow my rig."

"Merci. I would like to bury my friend tonight."

"That's a good idea. In this heat…."

Harper said, "Shut up, Moseby."

"I'm just saying."

"Get that wagon for this fellow."

The man in the back of the crowd rushed off. Montreur stood up. "Please, stand back. I will take charge of my friend."

Harper said, "Get on inside, men. You got drinking to do." After they left, he said, "I thought it best we clear the streets. There's no use having a bunch of curious coyotes hanging around."

"Oui." Montreur stepped between Harper and Brodie. "You have customers to tend to. I will handle my friend."

A wagon approached from down the street. "I will bury my friend. And then I will mourn."

"What about the law. I mean, this ain't no common bar fight. A killin' has to be reported."

"I will leave that to you, my friend."

"I'll telegraph the sheriff and see everything gets taken down proper. Somebody will pay for this. I promise."

The man with the wagon arrived. Montreur refused the man's offer of help and loaded Brodie into the bed of the wagon on his own. He covered the young man with a dirty blanket he found in the bed. After he tied the horses to the rear of the wagon, the owner put his foot on the rear wheel of the wagon. "How do I know you'll be bringing my wagon back, mister?"

Harper stepped over. "This man pays his debts. If he don't, I'll cover your expense."

"Merci. I shall be back in a day, two at the most." He offered his hand and the men shook. Montreur tied their horses to the back of the wagon, stepped up into the seat, and headed out of town. He looked back to the wagon owner. "Two days. No more."

"Aw right. Aw right." The man waved him off.

Montreur rode out of town at a fast pace and soon disappeared into the darkness. He turned once to look at the young man in the back of the wagon.

"Imbecile!"

24

Montreur drove the wagon several miles out of town at a fast pace. Once well out of sight of the town he pulled off the main road and hurriedly drove behind a small hill where he stopped, jumped out of the wagon, and rushed to his horse where he grabbed one of his bags. He hopped on the wagon bed and jerked the blanket off Brodie. Brodie's breathing was shallow, almost unnoticeable.

He felt the young man's right leg and found the bullet hole. He ripped open Brodie's pants with his knife and doused the wound with flour from a sack in one of the bags. The bleeding slowed. "Food and medicine, all the same." He tied off the wound and ripped off Brodie's shirt. Even in the dark he could see the wounds. The bullet in his left shoulder was a through-and-through. He poured more flour on the wounds and plugged them with cloth strips ripped from Brodie's shirt.

A small hole in his right side was also a through-and-through, the damage more painful than deadly – had the young man been conscious. He powdered and plugged this wound. The bullet that had hit his right shoulder was lodged in bone and he could feel it with his finger. He looked to the heavens. "Le Bon Dieu. Let this boy live." Montreur pulled a lucifer from his vest pocket, lit it and ran it along the cutting edge of his knife. He bent over and found the bullet in Brodie's shoulder, pinched it between his fingers and cut open the skin. The bullet, lodged in bone, would not be pinched out. "Sacre!" He bent over, bit the bullet and pulled it out with his teeth. He spit it over the side of the wagon and treated the wound.

The head wound, bleeding profusely, was the least dangerous of all. Montreur wiped it as clean as he could and wrapped a bandage around Brodie's head. He pulled the blanket back over his friend, left the bed, and climbed back into the seat. A moment later he was back on the road. He kept on going west. A few miles out of town he turned north toward the river and rode on in the light of false dawn until he found a flat area near the river. The view of the selected site was blocked from the road by a small hill. He pulled under a couple of cottonwoods which would provide cooling shade during the day. "Not much of a hospital, my imbecile friend, but it will have to do.

He dug shoulder and hip holes in the soft sand, placed the dirty blanket over them and then moved Brodie in. He untied the horses and hobbled them nearby before returning to his friend. Brodie's breathing was irregular and shallow. Montreur stayed with him that night, the next day and the next night. He cleaned and dressed the young man's wounds again. During the rare moments when Brodie was conscious, the old man made him sip some broth he had prepared from a few cuts of beef jerky. That second day he tied his horse to the rear of the wagon and rode back into Duncan.

He returned the wagon and was headed back out of town when Harper rushed out of his saloon. "Mr. Montreur!"

Montreur nodded, but kept riding.

"Stop, sir. We have to talk."

"I must be getting on."

"I need some information. For the sheriff when he comes. It's important."

Montreur stopped and dismounted. He followed Harper into the saloon. "This won't take long, Mr. Montreur."

"Montreur, just Montreur."

Harper poured a shot and a beer. "On the house, of course."

"Merci."

"I have all the information about the shooting, such as it is. Ah, about the young man, Brodie was his name?"

"Yes."

"And his last name?"

"Duphrane."

"And, ah… well, about the disposition of the body… I have to ask you understand."

"I buried my friend far in the desert. He sleeps under the stars."

"And where might that be?"

"I doubt if I could find it myself. Besides, my friend, he would not like his rest to be disturbed."

"Of course. Of course. Well, enjoy your drink."

"It is difficult to enjoy the death of a friend."

"Yes, Sir. As best you can."

"If you will excuse me, I must go mourn properly for my friend."

Montreur finished his drink and walked out of the saloon.

Montreur left Duncan at a relaxed pace, but once he climbed the plateau and was no longer in sight, he raced west as fast as he dared until he reached the camp. Brodie sat up under a tree right where he had left him. The younger man held a pistol in his hand. He was unconscious and very pale. Montreur tied his horse to a small tree and rushed to Brodie's side.

"Brodie."

Brodie opened his eyes. "Bear... heard him last night and pulled myself up... where...."

Montreur took the pistol and placed it in the nearby holster. "All is well, my friend. Rest."

Brodie nodded and closed his eyes. While he slept Montreur took the horses down to the river to drink. Later he rubbed down his exhausted animal with handfuls of dried grass. He rounded up more firewood and prepared coffee and broth. Brodie was able to get down a bit of each. Montreur checked his friend's wounds, cleaned and rebandaged them.

"Ca m' etonne! Most men would be dead of such wounds."

Brodie moaned, but said nothing.

"Rest. Sleep, imbecile. It is the best medicine."

That day set the pattern for most of the next week. Brodie slept, ate and drank a little while Montreur maintained the camp and used his medical skills to care for his patient. Brodie slowly gained strength and managed to sit up for longer periods of time, but was far too weak to walk.

"What happened, Montreur?"

"Betrayal."

"Who?"

"It could be anyone. You talk too much. Vengeance must be a silent thing – at least until you strike."

Brodie continued to heal and a few days later was able to walk. One evening he limped toward the river and joined the old Cajun who was sitting on a rock. A setting sun turned the cliffs and mountain sides yellow, gold and finally a deep orange.

"Thinking about those swamps of yours back home?"

"This is home."

"You aren't ever going back?"

"I have been back. Louisiana, the South, she is old, worn smooth like a pebble in the river. She no longer has rough edges."

"I think I understand."

"Perhaps. Someday, you, you and that girl of yours will smooth down even these rough edges." He pointed to the rugged mountains.

"That doesn't seem hardly possible."

"It is the way of things. Until then...." He gestured to the ragged rocks turning deep red in the sun's dying glow.

They sat in silence for a long time. The sky turned dark blue and then black as the stars popped out. Brodie picked up a handful of pebbles and tossed them one at a time into the approaching darkness.

"It was Tule Henderson who shot me, wasn't it?"

"Him or someone doing his bidding."

"I'm in no shape to go after him."

"No."

"He's won."

"Again, no."

"What do you mean?"

"This retribution, do you still seek it?"

"Yes, but there's more to it. That gold will give Enid and me...."

"Do not lie to me, my friend. And do not lie to yourself. You ride the vengeance trail."

Brodie paused and then threw the rest of the pebbles into the night. "Yes. And I pretty well messed that up."

"Perhaps. Vengeance requires patience. Are you a patient man, Brodie?"

"I can be."

"Can you ride tomorrow?"

"Some."

"Good. We will leave this place."

"We?"

"I cannot abandon you now."

"You've done more than your share of paying me back, Montreur."

"Perhaps. But I will remain at your side for a bit longer."

"Where are we going tomorrow?"

"North into the Black Hills."

"That's not Henderson's territory."

"Exactement. You are not ready for a confrontation, right?"

"I'm not rightly sure I'm ready for the Black Hills."

"We will take our time. You will heal. And, if you wish, you will have your vengeance. And perhaps the gold for that woman of yours."

"I appreciate… why are you sticking around?"

"Let us say that I wish to see the resurrection."

"Whose resurrection?"

"Yours, my young friend."

"I don't understand."

"You are dead, Brodie."

"I—"

"The men in Duncan all saw your body. The world, Tule Henderson, they all think you are dead. That, my friend, is a great advantage for someone seeking vengeance."

Brodie frowned and then smiled. "I'm a dead man."

"Oui. But you are a dead man who must heal before he returns to the trail."

"As a dead man, I have that time."

"Oui."

"Where are we headed then?"

"To see a buttercup."

25

Buttercup Beaudine was one of the most successful merchants in Hillsboro, New Mexico Territory. She loomed large in the expanding commercial enterprises and had financial interests in several gold mines, a couple of ranches, the largest mercantile store in the area, and a few other business enterprises. At 225 pounds, she loomed large in a physical way, too. Her most successful business was located at the eastern end of town in a large, two-story brick house recently constructed to meet the growing needs of an expanding clientele. The bordello's front porch was lit up at night by a dozen red lanterns. Buttercup said she advertised this way at the command of Holy Word.

"The Lord Almighty done said not to hide your light under no bushel basket and by god, the word of the Lord is good enough for me and my girls."

Most of the men of Hillsboro were honest and even those who weren't respected the trait when they saw it from afar. Buttercup was well-liked and respected for her business skills and admired for her large-size beauty. She used her come-on eyes and her seductive smile to enhance her attractiveness and, as one admirer said, "Makes bulk beautiful."

Brodie and Montreur arrived at her back door a week after leaving the Gila. Their travel had been slow due to Brodie's weakened condition, but the transition from dusty desert air to the cooler mountains and clear, spruce and pine scented breezes had a good effect. He spoke with more optimism even if his voice remained weak.

Montreur led Brodie in along the edge of town, avoiding the road in and the streets through the busy community. They dismounted at the rear of the bordello where Brodie remained mounted as Montreur entered the rear door. He stayed inside a considerable amount of time, but when he returned, Buttercup and one of her girls was with him. Brief introductions were made and then they helped Brodie off his horse and led him to one of several small cabins set away from the main house. Buttercup handed a large key to the young woman. "Nola will see to your needs… most of your needs."

"My friend just needs time to heal," Montreur said.

"Well, if'n he spends any of that healin' time making the beast with two backs, that's extra."

"Thank you, Mademoiselle Buttercup."

She faked a blush. "I do love a man who talks fancy."

"Remember, if anyone should ask, my friend has the fever."

"Everybody at Buttercup's has the fever, Montreur." She smiled and shook her hips before turning and going back into the house.

Nola had already opened the door and helped Brodie inside. He sat at a table in a corner of the room as she made the bed. "I can bring ya'll some supper later if you don't mind pot luck."

"That will be fine, mademoiselle. Food and rest will help cure my friend's fever."

"Well, I'd best be going. If you men need anything, Buttercup wants you to ask for me." She left quickly.

Brodie was so weak from the journey that Montreur had to help him undress and crawl into the bed. He nodded his thanks, closed his eyes and was soon asleep.

Montreur hung up his friend's clothes. The Cajun had ridden into Silver City several days earlier when they camped just south of the city. He nosed around and picked up no information about Tule Henderson. He carried a new set of clothes for his friend when he left town – clothes without telltale bullet holes in them. He stretched and sat down. Later, a gentle rapping on the door awakened him from a day dream.

"It's me, Nola."

Montreur unlocked the door and the young prostitute came in with a large tray of food – a hearty soup, some bread, a few cookies and a small flask of whiskey. "Madam Buttercup says today everything is on the house. Tomorrow…."

"I understand and I will thank her personally."

"She is a great lady."

"In many ways, Nola, in many ways." He looked over the tray with a pleased look on his face. He looked up to the young woman. "You said, I believe, 'everything' is on the house?"

"Everything on the plate is on the house."

They looked at each other for a few seconds. Nola was the first to speak. "There is another cabin nearby. I have the key."

Montreur stood up, looked to his sleeping friend, to the meal on the tray, and back to the young prostitute. He grabbed the whiskey flask from the tray and placed his arm around Nola. He eased her toward the door. "I have lived a long and most extraordinary life. I was born back in the bayou country...." His voice trailed off as they walked to the small cabin next door.

When he returned, Brodie was sitting at the table eating the meal. "I saved you half."

Montreur sat down, smiling. He placed the nearly empty flask of whiskey on the table. "I saved you... some." He quickly dug into the meal.

"The soup's cold," Brodie said.

"I am warm."

Brodie laughed. "I thought I heard that Nola swishing by."

"She is most talented at swishing."

Brodie finished off the whiskey and when Montreur finished eating, he said, "I've been thinking."

"No, my young friend. You have not been thinking. That is why you are shot to hell."

Brodie sat back, looking shocked at the apparent hostility in his friend's voice.

Montreur continued. "I owe you and I will repay that debt – if you live long enough."

"I didn't know—"

"Oui! But a smart man, a man who lives, must know. You are at a place of choices, Brodie. Either choice... you must be smart whichever path you take."

"How do you see it, Montreur?"

"You can return to that girl of yours, your Enid. You can live a rancher's life, forget this Tule Henderson, and hope he forgets you. Or, you can continue to ride the vengeance trail."

"You know which way I'm going."

"Do you wish my help?"

"Hell, do I look like I can take on Henderson and his men?"

Montreur laughed, but there was little mirth in it. "In your present state you could not even take on Nola."

"Enid is the only woman for me."

"I am serious, Brodie. You must make difficult decisions and you must make them now."

"What decisions?"

"You have a great advantage over this Henderson if you will use it."

"What would this great advantage be?"

"You are dead, my friend. You are dead."

Brodie sat forward. "If Tule Henderson thinks I'm dead, he won't be looking over his shoulder for me."

"A significant advantage. You must use it wisely."

"I have to heal up first."

"I have been listening. Henderson does not often ride this far north. I think we will be safe here for a time."

"How long?"

"I do not understand."

"You know what I mean. How long until I'm healed up?"

"Three months, maybe four. Two more to get you back into shape."

"I have to telegraph Enid."

Montreur slammed his palm against the table. "Imbecile. You are dead and you must stay dead. No one must know."

"But Enid...."

"Your Enid will get you killed."

"She can keep a secret."

"Her voice maybe, but not her face. Her emotions will speak and someone will hear. We can tell no one. If Brodie Duphrane is to live, he must remain dead."

"That's hard, Montreur."

"That is the decision you face."

Brodie stood up. He wavered slightly, but was able to make his way back to the bed. He sat down on the edge and starred at the Cajun. Several moments passed. "I guess you already know the way I have to go."

"Oui, Brodie. You made your decision long before you realized it."

Brodie looked to the floor and then back to Montreur. "Brodie Duphrane is dead. My name is Bock."

"Bock?"

"Yeah, sure. Jason Bock."

"It is a good name."

"Call me Jase."

"I am pleased to meet you Mr. Bock."

"Jase."

They shook hands as if meeting for the first time.

Montreur settled in as Brodie prepared for bed. He looked exhausted with a pained look on his face.

"The girl?"

"Enid. How's she going to handle my dying?"

"When you have finished with this Henderson, when you have his gold, and when you return from the dead, then you will know." He walked to the door. "Rest, my friend. For the moment, I feel that Nola wishes to hear more about my fantastic life."

"Have a drink for me."

"To resurrection."

"To resurrection."

Part Four

26

Lightning flashed in the dark clouds blowing in from the west as Brodie drove the battered old wagon into Cliff, a small farming and ranching town northeast of Silver City. He stopped at Stanbrough's Mercantile and with some effort stepped down and into the store. The owner greeted him with a smile and a brief wave of his hand. "How ya' doing, Mr. Bock?"

"Tolerable, Mr. Stanbrough, tolerable."

"Well, I've seen you worse."

"That you have."

"I'm glad to see you're up 'n running even if you are running a bit slow."

Brodie sat down in one of the chairs near the stove in the center of the store. "We'll need the usual."

Stanbrough nodded and began filling a couple of sacks with assorted goods. "Where's that crazy Cajun friend of yours? He usually comes in for your supplies."

"Hillsboro. I think he's gone sweet on one of Buttercup Beaudine's hostesses."

"He wouldn't be the first."

"He's what they call *smitten* I think."

Stanbrough stopped packing one of the sacks. "You want me to light a fire in there for you?"

"Thanks, but no use burning up your wood just for me."

"Bah. No trouble for good customers. And I know that fever of yours hasn't quite let go."

"Takes time."

"That it does." Stanbrough went back to filling the sacks. When he finished, he placed them on the counter. "On account?"

Brodie stood up. "Yeah. Montreur will come in and settle up at the end of the month."

Stanbrough helped Brodie carry the sacks out to the wagon. He said, "You folks finding any color out there? If you don't mind me asking?"

"Some. Not enough to make us rich. Too much to let us go."

"Well, you folks are due for a break. You've been out there, what, four months?"

"More like five, damn near six."

"You're a couple of persistent cusses, I'll give you that."

Brodie laughed. "Have to. All our profits go with Montreur over to Hillsboro. Brodie loaded the sacks onto the wagon, grunting with the effort to disguise the pain.

"You ought to see Doc Marsten about that fever."

"It's just something I have to ride out. And speaking of riding out...."

Stanbrough waved him off.

Brodie moved through town slowly and pulled up to a stop in front of the telegraph office. He stared for a moment at the front door, looked up and let his eyes follow the wires that connect the small town to the rest of the world.

"Oh, Enid."

He shook his head, snapped the reins and moved on out of town.

27

Brodie reined in at the Gila ferry a few minutes later. The water was rising slowly from rainstorms up river and the current was already becoming swift in the narrow body of water. The ferry was tied up on the far side. It was an old scow with a deck of rotting wood and a pilot house that was nothing more than a tattered canvas held up by four crooked cottonwood poles. A ramp for wagons was in place, but the ferryman was not in sight.

He brought his hand to his mouth and shouted. "Puerco!"

A young Mexican popped his head up from the bottom of the scow, awakened more by a loud clap of thunder nearby than by the shouting. He waved and grinned. Brodie waved him over and the young man quickly pulled in the ramp and began pulling the ferry across the river. He beached the craft and pulled out the ramp before running over to take Brodie's horses by the reins.

"Senor Bock. Back so soon?" Brodie tossed him a coin and Puerco led the horses up the ramp. The craft bobbled as the wind from the leading edge of the coming storm churned the waters. Puerco pocketed the coin and began pulling the ferry toward the other side of the Gila. Brodie grabbed the rope to help, but the young Mexican stopped him. "No, Senor Bock. You are ill. Wait in your wagon and I will get us across."

Brodie sighed. "I guess I'd not be much help anyway." He climbed aboard his wagon and watched Puerco move to the front of the boat and take the large rope in hand. Brodie jumped at a large flash of lightning and an ear-shattering clap of thunder tossed him off the seat and back into the bed of the wagon. He struggled to pull himself up and looked over the seat. Puerco was gone. Heavy rain hit as Brodie climbed down and worked his way to the front of the ferry.

"Puerco!"

He looked around, but couldn't see the boy.

Someone running along the shoreline and pointing down river shouted. "There!"

Brodie followed the man's lead and noticed something floating in the middle of the river – Puerco. He was face down and nearly submerged. "No!" Brodie pulled off his boots and tossed them and his hat in the bed of the wagon. He jumped into the water and started swimming down river. The foolishness of his actions struck him as brutally as the cold, rushing waters of the Gila. "Oh, Christ!" He swallowed water and coughed as the current took him under. His clothing became an anchor dragging him down. He flayed his arms and fought his way to the surface, bursting through and gasping for air.

The man running along the western shore threw a rope between Puerco and Brodie. The young Mexican continued to float face down, making no movement. *He's gone*, Brodie thought. *And I'm next.* His right hand found the rope and Brodie quickly wound it around his forearm, knowing he was too weak to hold on to it by hand. "Pull me in!" He rolled over, swallowed more water, righted himself and desperately held on to his lifeline.

Downriver, Puerco's body was pulled under. He did not resurface.

The man on the shore pulled as Brodie was taken further down river. The movement stopped with a jerk. He looked up to see that another man had joined the first. They were pulling him toward the shore. As he approached the shoreline his feet found loose footing and he was soon able to help his rescuers. He walked the last few steps in the river, but slipped and fell. He hit his head on a submerged rock, staggered forward on hands and knees and collapsed on the shore. The two men rushed to his side.

"You crazy sumbitch. That's the Gila, man."

"Leave him alone, Bozeman. He was just trying to save the kid."

"Committing suicide is what I call it. C'mon. Let's pull him out yonder."

Bozeman, and his partner, named Rackham, dragged Brodie to an open, grassy space. Lightning was still a danger, so they hunkered down in an open area to avoid the danger of a lightning strike on one of the sheltering trees nearby. Rackham held his large coat open to provide some shelter for the nearly-drowned man. Bozeman slapped Brodie several times on his face.

"Come on, Mister. Cough it up."

"That's Bock, that crazy Cajun's partner."

"Bock, snap out of it."

Brodie opened his eyes. He rolled over and threw up.

Bozeman said, "Good, Bock. Spit it out."

Brodie threw up again. He tried to sit up, but fell back.

"We better get him to the cabin," Rackham said.

"What about that wagon?"

"I'll pull it in. You two go on."

They helped Brodie to his feet. Rackham supported him as they walked away. Bozeman jogged up river and eventually pulled the ferry to shore. He climbed on board and crawled through the wagon. He examined all the sacks and, finding nothing of value, climbed into the seat and drove the horses off the ferry and toward the cabin he shared with Rackham.

The door to the cabin had been blown open by the wind. Rackham eased the unconscious Brodie through and gently dropped him on one of the two beds which were just large canvas bags stuffed with corn shucks and dry brush. Rackham began undressing his unexpected guest.

"I ain't getting familiar, Bock, but you're soaking wet and that ain't none too good for what's left of your health. He pulled of Brodie's boots, jacket, and pants, checking the pockets of each garment. He found a few coins and pocketed them. "I guess you lost 'em in the river, eh?" Rackham gasped when he removed Brodie's shirt and saw the scarred-over bullet holes.

"Damnation!"

Bozeman rushed in and kicked the door shut. He shook the rain off and hung his hat on a peg in the wall. "How is he? You find anything?"

"He's breathing. I got a couple of coins. It ain't much for the rescue, but it'll do." He pointed to Brodie's body. "Look at this."

"God Almighty. Who shot the hell out of him?"

"It don't matter none. But that 'fever' he's been having these past months wasn't due to no sickness." He grabbed a blanket and placed it over Brodie. The unconscious guest moaned, but did not wake up. "We better get Doc Townsend to look at him."

"I'll go as soon as the river gets quiet."

Bozeman squatted down. "What we got here is some kind of mystery."

Rackham took a bottle of whiskey from a shelf and took a drink. He handed the bottle to his partner. Bozeman stood up and drank. "The question is – what are we going to do with it?"

28

Montreur returned two days later and passed through town just as the business day began. When he passed the mercantile store, Stanbrough rushed out and called his name.

"What is it, Stanbrough?" He reined in his horse.

"It's your friend, Bock. He's in jail."

"Jail!"

"Yes, sir, and he's dinged up pretty bad, too."

"What is the accusation?"

"Murder."

"Bah!"

"This is serious, Montreur. You better get over there and see him. Tie up here. I'll watch your critter."

Montreur dismounted and handed the reins to the store owner. "Details, please. Speak quickly. You say he was hurt?"

"Banged his head up down at the ferry."

"And murder?"

"They say he killed that ferry operator, Puerco. Shot him in the gut and kicked him in the river the day before yesterday, he did. I mean, that's what they say. The marshal grabbed him just this morning."

"Who says this lie?"

"Those two bums living down at the end of town, Bozeman and Rackham. They saw it all. So they say."

"This was two days ago?"

"Yeah."

"And he was arrested only today?"

"That'd be right."

"Why the delay?"

"Like I said, he was dinged up pretty bad. Doc Townsend patched him up."

"The doctor, he examined my friend two days ago."

"Yeah, I think he's going to be all right. At least—"

"I will be back in a very few moments."

"Take your time." He stepped closer. "You watch your step, Montreur. Something about this just isn't right. I don't like it."

"We shall see what the facts tell us, eh?"

"There's facts and then there's the law. You watch your back."

Montreur turned and walked down the street.

The Cliff jailhouse was a reconstructed blacksmith shop that had burned down. The jail itself was just a large anvil left in place when the owner abandoned the property. Several long chains were affixed to the anvil and Brodie was affixed to one of those chains. Marshal Iverson sat in a chair at a desk at the opposite end of the building. He sat forward when the old Cajun stepped in. "I figured on seeing you pretty soon, Montreur."

Brodie sat up. His head was bandaged, but he was alert.

"I would like to see my friend… alone, if possible."

"Not possible, but you can whisper if'n you want to. I gotta check you for guns."

Montreur opened his coat to reveal a pistol stuck in his waist band. Iverson took the pistol. "Nothing personal."

Montreur punched Iverson in the solar plexus and the man doubled over. Montreur struck him twice more. Iverson fell over and dropped the gun. Montreur picked it up and struck Iverson on the back of the head.

"No offense."

Brodie jumped up. "What the hell?"

"We must run, my friend, and we must run very fast."

Montreur found the key to the cuffs on the chains and freed his partner. "Iverson's horse is out back. Take it and meet me at the cabin. Move!"

"That's horse thieving."

"So they will hang you twice."

"What—"

"Pack what you can and be ready. I shall follow."

"I didn't kill that boy."

"Go!"

Brodie walked quickly to the back door, opened and looked through it. He stepped outside and within seconds Montreur heard the sound of retreating hoof beats. He dragged Iverson to his chair and sat him in place. He put the newspaper in Iverson's hands and titled his head forward, which gave the appearance of a man who had nodded off. Montreur left the office and casually walked to his horse. Stanbrough was sweeping the wooden sidewalk.

"How's Brock?"

Montreur mounted his horse. "He will be fine."

"I guess you never know about some men."

"My friend is innocent. Remember that." Montreur rode away.

29

Brodie arrived at the cabin. His horse was missing. *Bozeman or Rackham – horse thieves*, he thought. He dismounted and patted Iverson's horse. *And now I'm one of 'em.* He moved inside and began packing: rifles, pistols, ammunition, slicker, blanket, and a few other necessities. The sound of hoof beats approaching quickly caught his attention. He walked to the front door, grabbing a rifle along the way and lowering when he saw Montreur ride up and dismount.

"Are you ready to run for your life, Brodie?"

"What the hell is going on?"

The Cajun leaned back against the wall as if he hadn't a care in the world. "Perhaps I could make us a pot of tea. And we can sit around and pass a good time discussing matters of great import… until the posse arrives bringing the rope that will end your foolish life under the nearest tree."

"All right. Let's move."

"Quickly."

A moment later the two fugitives had disappeared into the forest. Montreur led the way south, far around Cliff, but generally following the path of the Gila. He seemed confident of their way, but often Brodie saw no evidence of a trail, not even a faint animal run. Yet, they made good time, stopping about two hours before sundown to rest the horses and eat antelope jerky and some biscuits. When pushed, Montreur allowed Brodie to build a smokeless fire of dry wood, so they finished off the meal with hot coffee.

"Do we have time for that parlay now, Montreur?"

"You want to know why we run?"

"It's a good start."

"We run from Tule Henderson."

Brodie's eyes narrowed and he leaned forward. "Henderson?"

"You have a good heart, my friend, but you must learn how to think. How many people saw your body, your wounds?"

"Hell... Bozeman and Rackham, for sure. Then that doctor, Townsend."

"What does this mean?"

"I don't—"

"Think! I am trying to teach you something."

"If they saw all those bullet wounds they knew our story about my fever was all bull. So, they know we're up to something."

"And...."

"Oh, God."

"Yah. A man surviving with so many gunshot wounds is a known man. A man like Henderson pays money for such information."

"Rackham and Bozeman."

"Perhaps the doctor. Perhaps all three. Possibly that Marshal, too."

"How did you figure all this out so fast?"

Montreur poured the last drops of his coffee on the remains of the fire. He took the coffee pot and offered to pour for his friend. Brodie shook his head and Montreur dumped the contents onto the fire. He stirred the coals and kicked sand over them. The fire was soon nothing more than a hot mound of sand.

Brodie stood up and stretched. "How?"

"The delay. Puerco died—"

"I didn't do that."

"Of course not. But you were not arrested. You weren't even accused... not until after you wounds were seen. One of those men telegraphed the information to Henderson. This is his country. This murder charge is just an excuse to hold you, to hold you for killing."

"That means he knows I'm after him."

"Yes, my friend. The hunter is now the hunted."

Before they rode on, Montreur cleaned the site. After he finished, only an Indian or attentive scout would be able to recognize it as a stopping point on their journey. Late that afternoon a rain shower erased all the evidence. It was as if they had never been there at all.

30

The sun, yellow-white through the thin clouds began shining through pine and spruce as it eased down towards the shattered skyline of hills and valleys. Montreur leaned over looking forward and then sat upright in his saddle. "We camp now. I cannot follow this trail in darkness."

"Suits me."

They dismounted, unsaddled and hobbled their horses back a good distance from the animal run Montreur called a trail. The Gila rumbled down the rocky hillside. Brodie stood up and stretched. "I got to find the nearest necessarium."

"Pick your tree… downwind."

Brodie stepped across the camping area and walked to the edge of the rugged cliffs over the Gila. A slight movement caught his attention down at the river some thirty feet or so below. "Montreur! Get over here."

His partner jogged over. "What is it?"

He pointed slightly downstream. "A body. Look."

"Mon Dieu. This is a bad place to camp. We must move now."

"It's getting dark."

"The mountain lion and the bear, they like the dark."

"Yeah, let's—" Brodie blinked and leaned forward. "He's moving."

Montreur stepped forward and leaned over for a better look. The young man half in and half out of the water and face down in the dirt was dressed in light clothes. He had the dark hair and skin of a Mexican. His fingers clutched at the earth. Montreur moved quickly by following a natural break in the rocks. Animal scat along the way showed that others used the trail, too. Brodie followed. The arrived at the edge of the river and dragged the young man from the water.

Brodie turned him over. "Puerco!"

"I will be damned," Montreur said.

They pulled him further up onto a flat area covered with dry, brown pine needles. Puerco was about as busted up as a man could be and still be alive. His eyes flitted open.

"Senor Bock?"

"Yeah, Puerco. And Montreur, he's here, too."

Brodie looked to his partner and when they made eye contact Montreur shook his head. He stroked Puerco's hair.

The young man's voice was barely a whisper. "Mi familia."

"Your family, what about 'em?" Brodie asked.

Puerco reached slowly and with great pain into his shirt to a narrow canvas pouch tied around his waist. He pulled on it, but lacked the strength to do more.

"I'll get it, Puerco. All right?"

"Si."

Brodie pulled the canvas around Puerco's mid-section until he found a knot. He untied the bag. It jingled with coins. Some paper money was within it, too."

Puerco nodded. "Mi familia. For Rosa, for my Rosa, por favor."

Brodie said, "You want us to take this money to your family, right?"

"Si. My wife... the baby comes... soon."

"All right, Puerco. We'll see to it."

Montreur grabbed his friend's arm. "You do not know what you are saying, Brodie."

"Senor Bock...."

"Yes?"

Puerco let out a long slow final breath.

"We have to take him back," Brodie said.

"We cannot."

"It's the right thing to do. More than that, right here's proof that I didn't shoot him like they said. We can clear my name and I can get back to Henderson."

"If we go back, you will not live to see the end of the week."

"But Puerco… he hasn't been shot at all."

"You believe that is relevant?"

"The law says—"

"The law here is Tule Henderson. And he has pronounced you guilty."

Brodie sat back, staring at Puerco's body. "We have to bury him."

"The ground is rocky and we have no shovels."

"We can't just leave him like this."

"That we must."

"I won't leave a good man like this."

Montreur scanned the area. He pointed to a small cleft in the rocks about halfway up the hill. "There. It is the best we can do, my friend."

They struggled carrying Puerco's body to the cleft, stumbling several times and even dropping their burden once. The cleft was only a few feet deep, but it was fairly flat and long enough so that they could lay out the body.

"We should say some words," Brodie said.

Montreur took a deep breath. He placed his hands on Puerco's chest. "Bonne Chance. Adieu."

"What's that mean?"

"God speed. He is with his god now."

"I don't think so."

"You do not believe?"

"It's not that. If I was Puerco's spirit, I'd be with my woman. I'd be looking out for her right now."

"Perhaps. It is not an unheard of thing."

They looked at the young man for another minute or so. Montreur said, "We must go now and move our camp. We will back trail a safe distance."

"The animals, they'll take Puerco."

"As they will with each of us. Come."

They scrambled back up the hill, broke camp and headed back up the trail.

A small grove of trees fifty yards or so off the trail provided a secure camp site. "We're lucky you found this. I can't see more than a few yards in this darkness," Brodie said.

"There was no luck in this. Brodie, I am trying to teach you important things. Look where you go. Always. And remember. I noted this and many others as we rode through."

"I'm a rancher, not a Mountain Man."

"You are a fugitive. You must become a survivor." Montreur pulled his blanket up to his neck as he leaned against a pine tree. "The money, you will take it to that unfortunate young man's family."

"Of course."

"You realize the danger in such a foolish action."

"She's a woman and she needs protecting."

"And so do you." He closed his eyes, ending all conversation for the night.

31

Gila was a community similar to Cliff, but much smaller. Any strangers entering town attracted immediate attention and comment. Brodie and Montreur looked over the town from beneath the shelter of an Alligator Juniper on the top of a grassy hill. The Cajun scanned the town with a pair of binoculars. "This is ranching country. You should feel at home... until they hang you."

"Cajun humor?"

"Cajun reality."

"How the hell are we going to find Puerco's wife? We don't even know what she looks like."

"I do."

"Have you met her, seen her?"

"No. I have never laid eyes on the woman."

"Then how are you going to find her?"

"I look for a Mexican woman with child."

"I didn't think of that."

"Of course not; it is the obvious thing. I shall keep watch for a while. You tend to the horses."

"All right."

Brodie backed away on all-fours and then walked down the hill to a small grove of trees above a wash. The area was fairly well concealed and made for a safe place to hold up at least for a while. He hobbled the horses and placed the saddles under one of the trees. He waited a couple of hours before returning to the top of the hill. Just before reaching the crest he eased down and crawled back under the juniper. "Any luck?"

"Yes." Montreur handed over the binoculars. "Look to the general mercantile, the big store on the left halfway through town."

"And...."

"Wait." Montreur shaded his eyes and looked to town.

Several moments later a dark skinned woman with shiny black hair stepped out of the mercantile store. She wore a colorful skirt and a plain white blouse. She was pregnant and obviously very near her delivery time.

"You think that's her?"

"I have seen no other women with child down there. Watch where she goes."

The woman carried her small burden of sacks down the street to a small adobe structure off by itself at the far end of town.

"That has to be her," Brodie said.

"Because that is the way you want it to be. But I think you are right, but we must wait and observe more. Then we can act."

"Any idea as to just what the hell that act might be?"

"Something quiet and without incident."

"Amen."

Brodie took the watch until well after sundown. When he returned to the grove of trees, Montreur was returning from checking on the horses. He said, "We will water them down at the river soon."

"I hated to leave them there all afternoon."

"We cannot risk daylight and being seen."

"You're right, but I don't like to see them suffer."

"Suffering is living. Come. It is time."

They saddled the horses and slowly and carefully made their way to the river where the horses drank their fill.

"Now what," Brodie said.

"Now we wait for a while and then we go calling."

The Gila saloons were busy and rowdy, but the far end of town where Puerco's wife lived was quiet and dark. Brodie and Montreur rode up, tied off their horses and knocked on the door to the one-room adobe home. A young woman, not pregnant, opened the door. A heady aroma of beans and smoked pork followed her words. "May I help you, Senors?"

Brodie opened his mouth to speak, but Montreur spoke first. "Is this the home of Puerco's woman?"

The woman took half a step back and a touch of fear registered in her eyes. "Si. But he is not here."

"We know, Senorita. May we come in?"

"It would not be proper."

"Leave the door open. We have important news."

"A moment, please." She shut the door. They heard a brief conversation within, but could not make out the words. When the woman opened the door again, she motioned for them to enter. The door stayed open after they stepped inside. Puerco's woman sat near the fireplace where she stirred a pot of stew. The younger woman said, "This is Maria. She is Puerco's wife. I am her sister, Paulita. Who are you?"

"My name is Bock," Brodie said.

"Montreur," Madam.

"And your business?"

Maria spoke up. "Paulita, we have guests." The two women looked at each other. Maria nodded.

Paulita said, "If you are hungry, we have plenty."

Brodie said, "That would be most generous, Ma'am. But first I think you ought to hear our news. You... Maria there might feel different when she hears what we have to say."

Maria said, "It is Puerco, is it not?"

"Yes, Ma'am."

"He comes?"

"No, Ma'am." Brodie lowered his head and then looked back up. "I am afraid he will never come."

Paulita eased over and placed her arms on her sister's shoulders. "He is dead?"

Brodie nodded.

Maria said, "You are certain."

"We laid him to rest just yesterday. We said some words over him."

The two sisters looked at each other. Paulita's lips formed a brief smile. Maria drew in a breath and exhaled. The act seemed to take some heavy burden from her shoulders. Her drawn face relaxed and she patted her sister's hand. "Please sit down, Senors. Your news is welcome."

Paulita said, "You bring the answer to many prayers." She set the table for four and served the pork, beans and tortillas with mugs of water dipped from a covered jug. They ate in near silence for a few moments.

Paulita cleared her throat. "Our reaction to your news, it must seem strange."

Montreur said, "It is not as we expected, that is true."

Paulita said, "Puerco was—"

Maria placed her hand on her sister's hand. "Puerco was for a time a good man. A little wealth can change that. Puerco earned his little wealth with that ferry in Cliff. He stayed more and more in that accursed village. When he returned, now and then, he was violent."

"He had another woman. Rosa, I think," Paulita said.

Maria ever so slightly raised her hand. "It is true. I have not seen him in many months, not since I began showing." She patted her belly.

"Sangler. A man should not so burden his woman," Montreur said.

Brodie rapped the table lightly with his knuckles. "There is something else. You're going to hear that I killed Puerco. It's not true. He died in an accident on that ferry of his. Over in Cliff they say I shot him. I swear, Ma'am, that is not so."

Maria looked into his eyes. "I believe you, Senor."

Montreur said, "You can believe him, Ma'am. I wasn't there when it happened, but… without getting into unpleasant details, I know for a fact it's true."

When they finished, Paulita cleared the table. Maria said, "Of course, you cannot stay the night here, but you are welcome to sleep out front next to my home. The shade under the roof is most comfortable in the morning. Paulita and I will prepare breakfast.

Montreur said, "That's generous, Ma'am.

Paulita made coffee and the four spoke without saying much at all for about an hour. Montreur at last said, "We should bed down. We must be moving before sunrise."

Maria said, "We rise early here. You will not leave hungry."

Brodie and Montreur spoke very little as they bedded down. The two tired and very full men were soon asleep.

The black shadows of night were just beginning to turn gray in the light of pre-dawn when Brodie was awakened by a kick to his feet. He reached for his pistol.

"Hold it, mister." The voice was followed by the sound of a pistol being cocked. Brodie looked up. Montreur was sitting up, his hands in the air. Five armed men stood above them. Four were wearing uniforms.

32

Brodie and Montreur stood up, hands in the air.

One of the uniformed men, a sergeant swung his pistol back and forth from Brodie to Montreur and back to Brodie and, said, "Cotton, are these the two?"

An older man not in uniform stepped up, but before he could approach the prisoners the door opened. Maria and Paulita held candles. "What is the meaning of this intrusion," Maria said.

The sergeant said, "Apologies, Senora, but we need to talk to these two men.

"These men are my guests and this is my home."

The sergeant stepped forward, but kept his distance from his two prisoners. "Sergeant Atwood, Senora, I am out of Fort Bayard." Atwood was a large black man, a buffalo soldier, with an expression that left no doubt as to who was in charge of the situation. He pointed to the man called Cotton. "This man said two fugitives, killers, were hold up here."

Montreur said, "Does this have the appearance of holding up, Sergeant?"

"Privates Wesson and Stockton."

"Yes, Sergeant."

"Watch these men. If they move, shoot them."

"Yes, Sergeant."

Atwood spoke to Montreur. "You may lower your arms." He turned to Maria. "Your guests may be outlaws, murderers perhaps."

"I think not, Sergeant."

"I'm in the Army. I ain't paid to think." He tilted his head over his right shoulder, but kept his eyes on Maria. "Cotton! Get up here."

An old man dressed head to toe in dark, greasy buckskins stepped up. He was a throwback to a nearly forgotten era, the age of the Mountain Man.

Atwood spoke to Maria. "Excuse us for a moment, Senora. Please step back inside."

She nodded, backed away and closed the door. Atwood looked at the scout, who had not moved a step closer. "Well, are these the men?"

"Yep, sonny. I seen 'em sneakin' around town all of yesterday. Knew they was up to no good, I did. That's when I come back to get you soldier boys. They got to be them murderers from over Cliff way."

The gray of false dawn was giving way to the light blues and deep orange of a rising sun. Montreur leaned forward and looked at the old man. "Meneur! Liar." He turned to Atwood. "This man you call Cotton, is Loosem' Cockram."

Two of the buffalo soldiers, older men, smothered laughs. Atwood bellowed, "What is so funny, privates."

Before they could speak, Montreur said, "Allow me, Sergeant. I believe I can educate you as to the quality of your guide."

"Educate, Mr...."

"Montreur, just Montreur. My partner, he is called Bock."

The old Mountain Man starred at his accuser. "Montreur?"

Montreur stepped forward half a pace. The old scout backed away several steps. Loosem' Cockram has a scar shaped like an X on his right forearm. I gave it to him up on the Green River."

"And what will that prove?"

"That I speak the truth. And that this man is a liar."

Atwood kept his eyes on his prisoners, but spoke to his scout. "Cotton... or Cockram, show me your arm."

No, sonny boy."

"So, Montreur. He lies. You tell the truth... about a liar. I'm stuck in the middle and there is still the matter of this murder in Cliff."

Private Wesson stepped up. "Sergeant, I know this here Frenchy."

"Cajun."

Wesson grinned. "This here Cajun, I knowed him from Taos some years back. He's crafty, but he ain't the kind to lie about anything important."

Montreur said, "Long time, Joseph."

"Long time."

Atwood said, "I do not have time for this."

The man called Cotton spoke up. "You got to hold 'em, soldier boy. I got a reward coming for these two."

"Reward. There's not even a wanted poster on these men."

"I still got a reward coming."

"Who's paying this reward?"

"Mister... never you mind, soldier boy. Never you mind. You just bring these boys down to Lordsburg."

Atwood turned to the old Mountain Man. "Mister Cotton, or Cockram, you will address me as Sergeant or Atwood or Sergeant Atwood. But if you call me boy again I will have you skinned." He turned back to Maria. "Senora, we will pay you for coffee and beans if that is acceptable."

"Si, of course."

"May we also have use of your kitchen table?"

"Si."

Atwood looked to his men. "We'll rest here for a while. Wesson, you take care of things out here. Cotton, Montreur, Bock, you come with me and let's settle this confusion." The four men entered Maria's home. She and Paulita busied themselves preparing beans, tortillas and coffee. Atwood gestured for the other men to sit. "Cotton here came to me yesterday saying something about two killers being holed up in Gila."

"Bock is no killer and neither am I, Sergeant," Montreur said.

"And Cotton isn't Cotton, is that right?"

"Liam Cockram, Loosem' Cockram, the worst guide in the Rockies. Don't turn your back on him, Sergeant."

Cotton pulled a knife and moved toward Montreur. Atwood drew his pistol and Cotton stopped and backed up.

Montreur said, "A wise move Cockram." He loosened his grip on the Bowie knife halfway out of its sheath. He let the blade slide back and then sat back.

"Talk," Atwood said. He looked at the man called Cotton. The old man said that he had gotten wind of the murder while in Cliff. When he rode over to Gila he had noticed two men acting like suspiciously and, good citizen that he was, he tracked down the soldiers to help bring them in. Atwood then asked for Montreur's version of the events. He listened, but did not comment. When the explanations were over, he stood up. "My men are hungry and tired. They will occupy this table now. Follow me." He walked out of the home. The other followed.

Atwood spoke to his men. "The senora is just about ready with that breakfast. Eat hearty. Eat fast. We move out soon."

The soldiers stepped inside without comment.

"Wesson, stay here a moment.

"Yes, Sergeant."

"You say you know this man, Montreur?"

"From way back."

"And you trust him?"

Wesson smiled at Montreur. "I wouldn't say that, Sergeant, but he ain't known to be a liar. If he says something, you can bank on it."

Atwood looked to Cotton. "Cotton or Cockram, who is offering this reward and how did you hear about it?"

"To hell with you, boy."

Atwood quickly pulled his pistol and aimed it at Cotton's head. He spoke to Wesson. "Private, take this man past the edge of town and skin him."

"Yes, Sergeant." Wesson grinned and put his hand on his knife.

Cotton backed away, stumbled, and backed away farther.

Atwood said, "Go collect that reward of yours."

"You're gonna pay for this, boy."

"Git!"

Cotton mounted his horse. He leaned forward and looked directly at the two women standing nearby. "You'll see me again." He turned and rode back to Gila, cursing all the way.

"Wesson."

"Yes, Sergeant."

"You brought that man into camp. Do you know him?"

"No to Cotton. If he's really that Cockram fellah, I've heard plenty 'bout him and ain't a bit of it good."

"One last time, Private, what do you know about these men?"

"I don't know the younger fellah, but me and old Montreur, we shared morn 'n our share of Taos lightning."

"Trust him?"

"Less'n you play cards or try to out drink him."

Atwood turned to Montreur and Brodie. "These are the cards I'm dealing. We can escort you back to Cliff... and Iverson."

Brodie said, "We can't do that, Sergeant."

"Etre dans le trouble. That is a death sentence for my friend."

Atwood paused before speaking. "Iverson is trouble; that's for sure. But you men are under suspicion, am I right?"

"Unjustly so, but yes," Brodie said.

"You will ride with us to Fort Bayard, then. We'll let the authorities fight it out while you're in U.S. Army custody.

Brodie shook his head. "I have business in Lordsburg."

"All right. In the morning we'll ride you over to Cliff. You can make your case to Iverson."

"Damn it! We'll ride to Bayard."

"Smart move."

Montreur laughed.

"What's so funny?"

"Sergeant, you are at a moment prestigious. My young friend makes a wise decision. It is something new in his experience."

33

Before leaving, Brodie and Montreur asked for a moment alone with Maria. Atwood agreed, but he placed Private Jacobs near the door and insisted that the door remain open. Brodie untied Puerco's makeshift moneybag from his waist and handed the canvas bag to Maria. "I didn't know Puerco very well, Ma'am, so I don't pretend to know what kind of man he was. I do know that his dying thoughts were about his woman. He wanted me to get this money to you."

Maria looked startled as she accepted the bag and placed it on the table. The jingle of the coins sounded muffled in the room. "These coins will be a blessing. I am surprised."

"Those were his last words, Ma'am. To get this money to his woman."

"Perhaps there was some good left in him after all."

"Perhaps. Good luck to you, Ma'am." Brodie turned and walked out of the house.

Montreur placed his hat on his head. "The best of luck to you, Maria. You, too, Paulita."

"Vaya con Dios," Montreur.

Outside, Montreur said, "Puerco said to give the money to some Rosa."

"I don't know Rosa. Maria was good to us."

"Say no more. You did the right thing."

The other men were mounted. They joined them and with final wave to the women, the small party moved south. They rode slowly and easily. Privates Jacobs and Stockton took the lead. Atwood and Brodie rode next to each other. Montreur and Wesson rode drag and chattered like old friends.

Brodie said, "Are we under arrest?"

"No, not unless you cross the line." Atwood said.

"Where is that line?"

"You'll know when you cross it. For now, we need every man in this party armed and alert."

"Renegades?"

"Possibly. Bandits are becoming the big problem now that we've about rounded up the Apache."

"What happens when we reach Fort Bayard?"

"That's not up to me. You'll get a fair hearing. I promise that much."

"That's all I need."

They cut almost due south and covered about four miles before connecting with a halfway decent road that skirted the edge of what people were calling the Big Burro Mountains. The road paralleled a modest stream that gently turned southeast toward Silver City and Fort Bayard beyond. A few hours later the stream turned southwest. The road forked southeast and they followed it at a slow and easy pace for several miles until the sun began to set. Atwood signaled to make camp.

The soldiers shared their rations and also enjoyed biscuits and bacon provided by Maria and Paulita. The night air in the foothills was cool, so Atwood allowed a small fire. Atwood, Jacobs and Stockton spent the night near the fire. Montreur and Wesson left and split up; the Cajun slept deep in the shadows north of camp. Wesson found a comfortable recess near a rocky outcrop with a good view of the surrounding area. Brodie tended the fire until the soldiers were asleep and then found a place deep in the shadows east of camp.

Atwood awoke to the smell of burning pinion and boiling coffee. "Damn, Montreur, don't you make any noise?"

"Old habits, Sergeant."

Atwood sat up and stretched. He grabbed a small handful of pebbles and tossed them a couple at a time at Jacobs and Stockton. "Wake up, soldiers. We sleep in beds tonight." He looked around. "Where's Wesson. And your friend, Bock?"

"Bringing in breakfast I hope. Wesson and I set a few snares last night."

His hopes were fulfilled when Wesson and Brodie returned, each carrying a skinned and gutted rabbit hung on thin ropes. Without a word, Wesson made a spit while Brodie skewered the rabbits. The small group ate and drank and shared the last couple of Maria's biscuits. By the time the sun was close to reaching the tops of the nearby trees the men were mounted and headed east.

They rode without incident until about midday. Jacobs occasionally rode some distance ahead to scout out the road. Montreur and Wasson continued to ride drag. Occasionally, Montreur pulled off the road and into the protection of a stand of pinion just to watch their back trail. He always returned to Wesson with the same report. Apparently, they weren't being followed.

"I don't like it," he said.

Wesson said, "It has been a peaceful road. Do you remember them Ute's over in the Colorado?"

"The one's we thought weren't there? I can't hardly forget."

"I don't see nothing. I don't hear nothing. But... damn."

"Keep your nose to the wind."

Ahead Brodie eased closer to Atwood. "I have urgent business in Lordsburg, Sergeant."

"In due time, Mr. Bock."

"You could just look away for a minute. I'll take care of my business and then ride straight into Fort Bayard. Ask, Montreur. My word is good."

"And my mind is set. We'll clear this mess up good and proper Army style and then....". He sat up in the saddle. Jacobs raced toward them from a high ridge. He reined in his horse. Jacob had a worried look on his face. "Trouble, Sergeant."

"What kind of trouble, Private?"

"There's a wagon in the road about half a mile up ahead. It's been scattered all around. And there's been a fire... and a man tied to one of the wheels. I didn't go no closer."

Damn." Atwood raised his arm and signaled for the men to close in. When they did, he explained the situation. "We move in easy. Everybody stay alert."

The wagon and the scattered goods were in a depression in the road just beyond the ridge line, an area surrounded by trees and broken rock. The air smelled of burned wood and paper. Brodie said, "It's mighty curious they'd torture a man in the road like that."

Montreur said, "I agree, my friend. I do not like this."

Brodie and Montreur drew their pistols. Wesson waited, but looked to Atwood, waiting for a command. They were in hailing distance when the man tied to the wheel waved his wrists in the air. The movement was feeble.

Jacobs said, "He's alive, Sergeant, he's alive." Jacobs spurred his horse forward.

Brodie and Montreur shouted at the same time. "Stop!"

Jacobs reined in his horse and began to dismount when the man at the wheel turned. The ropes supposedly tying him down fell away as he reached into his britches and pulled out a .45 Colt. He fired three times. Two bullets struck Jacobs in his chest. The third blew a hole in his hand. The man turned and raised his pistol, pointing to Atwood. Brodie and Montreur fired at the same time. Four bullets struck the man's chest, knocking him back against the wagon. He slid down into the dust.

Other shots rained in from the surrounding rocks. Atwood shouted, "Cover! Get down!" He jumped from his horse and rushed to the nearest protection – the wagon. He stepped up on the wheel and threw himself inside. Bullets smacked into the sides, but did not penetrate.

Wesson and Montreur were already off their horses, rifles in hand. They split up with Wesson rushing into the safety of a jumble of rocks at the edge of the trail. Montreur zigged and zagged his way into a small wash about four feet deep. Brodie wheeled in a rapid circle and fired a couple of shots at the gun smoke rising from beneath a cluster of pinions. He dismounted as another shot from the opposite direction tore the pommel off his saddle. He rushed to the wash and rolled in next to Montreur. Stockton rode his horse to the wagon and jumped in. A bullet ripped into his thigh as he climbed over the side.

The shooting stopped and almost a minute passed before a man shouted from the far side of the road. "Looks like we got you in a little crossfire, eh, boy!"

"Cockram!" Montreur said.

"How the hell did he get ahead of us?"

"A man like that must know all the trails. And we have been traveling slow."

"What does he want?"

"Two things, I think. He wants to kill those black men. And, he wants you."

"Henderson again?"

"Who else."

Several shots exploded from each side of the camp. The dust piled up on the edge of the wash exploded over Brodie's head. Other shots struck the wagon.

"Atwood, you men hurt," Brodie shouted.

"Stockton's hit. Not bad. I'm all right."

Three shots hit the sides of the wagon.

Cockram shouted, "You're mine, boy. You're mine."

Another shot slammed into the wagon.

Brodie sat up, but kept his head well below the top of the wash. "How many?"

"Four guns, but I think only three men. Two on the other side and one back there."

"Yeah. I got a glimpse of the loner. He's behind some deadwood about fifty yards back. I think I can get him."

"You're a good shot, my friend, but...."

Brodie pointed up the wash. "This thing swings around and peters out back behind some pinons. I can work my way up there and get behind him – beside him at least."

A shot from Cockram's position kicked up the orange dust at the edge of the wash. Brodie said, "He's got you pretty well pinned down."

"Do not worry about me, Brodie."

"You know the sound of my rifle. When you hear it, don't worry about anything back this way. After, I'll circle around and we'll have them in a crossfire."

"Go."

Brodie crawled up the wash slowly and with great care to avoid kicking up any dust that might betray his movements. The wash narrowed and became continually shallower. He stopped beneath a small pinion growing at the edge. Dirt and debris kicked around by the wind had piled up around its base. He eased his head up behind this cover for a glance around. The shooter was easy to spot. The man rested half his body on a pile of sand under the low-hanging arms of a large pinion. He took aim at the wagon and fired. The shell hit one of the wheels and ricocheted into the hills. The man laughed and cocked his rifle for another shot. He remained in place.

Brodie moved swiftly and was up on his knees in seconds. He raised his rifle and fired. The bullet missed the shooter under the pinion, but it struck the man's rifle and knocked it spinning down the pile of dirt. The shooter looked up with a horrified, terrified look on his face. He spread his arms out, backed up several steps, and fell over. He turned over and fought his way up and began running away. He drew his pistol as he ran.

Brodie stepped out of the wash and followed.

"Damn!"

The land was a natural-color checkerboard of rugged boulders, pinion and pine, and dry washes. The shooter ran and stumbled again, but he didn't fall. He fired back toward Brodie without even looking. The shot was wide by more than a dozen yards. Brodie jogged along keeping obstacles between him and the runner as much as possible. He gained on the man without much effort.

When the shooter looked back a second time to fire another round he ran into a pinon and fell to ground. His gun fell into the dirt. While he scrambled in the dust for his weapon, Brodie used the distraction to jump behind some scrub brush. He had a perfect view of his enemy.

"It's over!"

The shooter raised his pistol and fired several shots, all of the wild. Brodie raised his rifle, aimed and fired. The shooter staggered back. He screamed like a frightened woman. Brodie fired again and a bullet tore into the man's chest. He looked down and began tearing at his jacket and shirt. He looked up and saw Brodie as a final bullet smacked into his chest. He fell over into the dirt. Brodie rushed up and examined the dead man. He took the pistol and the gun belt and continued back into the lightly wooded terrain.

He jogged on for a couple of hundred yards and then turned and jogged another hundred yards so that the ambush sight was slightly downhill and to his left. Cockram shouted several times – a question by the tone of his voice. Montreur shouted something back and fired a round in the direction of the voices.

"That's good, you old Cajun. Keep them sons a' bitches busy."

Brodie worked his way back toward Cockram's position below. He moved as quickly as possible when the wind kicked up to disguise the sound of his footsteps. When the wind died, he crawled and often gently shoved away small branches and twigs that might snap and betray his position. Montreur fired a round now and then. He saw Atwood raise up from the wagon bed to fire, but several shots slamming into the side forced him back without him firing a shot. Brodie entered a narrow wash cutting though the hill side. It provided some cover as he moved down toward the attackers. He was within about fifty yards when Cockram stood up behind a tree and cupped his hands to his mouth.

"Colored boy!"

"The name is Sergeant Atwood." The sergeant sounded defiant regardless of his position.

"I'll call you worse 'n that before I'm through with you, boy!"

Atwood popped up and fired three rounds from his pistol before dropping back into the wagon bed. All the shots were wild.

"You gotta do better 'n that, boy!"

Cockram laughed as he stepped from behind the tree. He spoke to the man hiding beside him. He looked back to the wagon. "Hey, boy. We figured you'd jump for that wagon if we didn't kill you outright. So, we made up some presents for you." Cockram placed his rifle against the tree. His partner handed him two whiskey bottles with strips of cloth stuffed in the necks. The man struck a Lucifer and lit each fuse. Cockram stepped out further.

"Ever been to Mississippi, boy?"

"Go to hell."

"Speakin' of hell...."

Cockram drew his hand back to throw the first bottle. Brodie's shot shattered the bottle and covered Cockram's head and torso with a liquid which immediately caught fire. He screamed and dropped the second bottle. It shattered against a rock and splashed more fluid and fire on the old man.

His partner stood up in horror. Montreur's shot blew half his head off. He fell back into the dust.

Cockram screamed, panicked and ran into the sparse pinion forest. He stumbled and fell, but landed on all fours. His agonizing screams reached a peak and then died to a whimper. Brodie took aim, but lowered his rifle. *I guess you won't be seeing Maria and Paulita again after all.* Cockram struggled, squealed weakly and fell into the dirt.

Brodie turned and walked back to the ambush site. Wesson and Atwood were bandaging Stockton's thigh wound.

"He'll make it," Atwood said.

Montreur walked the perimeter of the site, scanning the distance as if half-expecting another attack. He disappeared for a moment as he stepped into a wash down from the site. He returned a moment later. "There's a body down there. This'll be his wagon. A drummer I suspect from all this junk scattered about."

Atwood stood up. "We'll take him and Jacobs with us to Fort Bayard."

Brodie said, "The others?"

"What others?"

"Yeah."

Wesson left to round up the horses of their assailants. Brodie and Montreur walked down to the wash and brought back the body of the drummer. "Looks like they worked him over pretty good before they killed him," Brodie said.

"He took some time to die; that is certain."

"If they were going to kill him anyway, why...."

"For some men, the suffering of others brings joy."

"I don't understand."

Montreur said nothing until they placed the man's body in the wagon beside Jacobs. "I watched when you turned Cockram into a torch."

Brodie looked away.

"You could have put him out of his agony."

"He deserved what he got, Montreur."

"Ca c'est pour sur. That is certain, but...."

"But what?"

"That is probably what Cockram said about this poor man here."

Wesson returned. "They were riding pretty poor horseflesh, Sergeant. They ain't no good to us. I unsaddled and let 'em go."

Atwood nodded and motioned for the private to climb aboard.

As they rode away Brodie looked back over his shoulder. A small, steady column of black smoke rose through the pinion – a dark smudge fouling a clean, blue sky.

34

The sudden drop in adrenalin shortly after the firefight left the men tired.

Atwood noticed the drooping heads. "Stay sharp! Tired men get careless and careless men out here get killed fast."

They rode east without conversation. Montreur continued to drop out to watch their back trail, but no one followed. Atwood noticed each disappearance, but said nothing about it and did nothing to restrain the effort. Silver City was a busy hub of activity offering any distraction the weary traveler might desire, but they passed through without stopping. The low hills were sparsely covered with small trees and scrub brush and many places along the road offered ideal locations for ambush. Their progress was peaceful and the only encounters were with riders and wagons engaged in commerce.

When the road turned slightly northeast Atwood halted. "Montreur. Brodie." He rode back and gestured for the men to follow. He stopped just out of earshot of the men at the wagon.

"You men could have run during the fight and left us to Cockram."

"Not likely," Brodie said. His voice was clipped and held back a touch of anger.

"Oui," Monterur said.

"And you could have run out any time after the fight."

"What are you getting at, Sergeant?"

"I think you did us a good turn during an ambush. Afterwards, I think you two lit out. There was no way me and my men could follow, not with dead and wounded. So, you escaped. At least, that's what my report's going to say."

Brodie and Montreur looked at each other and then to Atwood.

Brodie nudged his horse forward. He stuck out his arm. "You're a hell of a soldier, Sergeant Atwood; I'd like to shake your hand."

Atwood said, "Well, if you was here, I'd be proud to do to that. But seeing that you're halfway to God knows where...." He smiled and turned away.

Brodie and Montreur watched as Atwood and his men rode away into the hills. They decided to camp instead of returning to Silver City. They built a fire about an hour before sundown and cooked up a pot of coffee, which they enjoyed with some canned peaches they had picked up from the dead drummer's goods. After eating, they covered the fire and moved on a couple of miles, finally settling in for the night after sundown.

"What do you think we ought to do now, Montreur?"

The old Cajun leaned back against a smooth rock and starred at the sky for a moment. "For me...."

"Go on."

"Hillsboro. I am partial to that lovely girl who works for Big Minnie."

"Nola."

"Her eyes shimmer like starlight on still waters."

"I never really looked at the lady's eyes."

"I got around to them, my friend... eventually."

They laughed and fell into silence for several minutes. Montreur finally spoke. "You must follow a more dangerous path, one that leads south to Lordsburg."

"And to Tule Henderson."

"You are each now hunters and the hunted. Only one can survive. Perhaps not even one."

"No, Sir. I didn't go through all this just to get myself killed."

"Again."

Brodie laughed. "I forgot. I'm a dead man aren't I?"

"An avenging angel perhaps."

"I like that."

"And then...."

"And then it's back to Mexican Hat."

"And that girl."

"Enid."

"She waits?"

"Of course."

"Hmm. I would not think of her until you have finished your business with Tule Henderson. Love is a dangerous distraction for someone seeking vengeance."

Brodie broke a thin twig and held half of it between his thumb and middle finger. He flicked it away using his index finger. The twig spun away and was lost in the darkness. "This will all be over soon."

"There is something else, my friend. Beware."

"Of what?"

"I have seen your dark self. Never forget that Lucifer was an angel, too."

When the pale light of sunrise broke through a crack in the mountains and caressed Brodie's face, he sat up and stretched. He looked around. Montreur and his horse were gone. Brodie stood up, stretched again and looked northeast toward Hillsboro. He waved toward the sunrise and to no one in particular. He gathered some dry wood and built a fire for coffee. When the sun finally cleared the tallest peak, Brodie rode out of camp and turned his horse southwest toward Lordsburg.

Part Five

35

"Tule Henderson's dead?"

"That's the rumor."

Brodie slumped and starred at Joe Dean Wilhite, bartender of the Mint Saloon in downtown Lordsburg.

"That can't be. Are you sure?" He unconsciously stroked the beard he had been growing for nearly half a year – a disguise.

Wilhite looked to the back of the room where a couple of cow-hands played billiards. They stopped playing and began chatting in low voices. Their eyes were on the two men at the bar. Wilhite lowered his voice. "Are you a friend of his?"

"Not exactly." He pointed to his shot glass. Wilhite poured. "Are you sure?"

"Like I said, Mister…."

"Bock, just Bock."

"Well, Mister Bock, I can't say from personal experience, but everybody in this neck of the woods thinks he took a pill in the stomach he couldn't digest."

The cowhands in the back of the room went back to their game. The clicking of the billiard balls punctuating their speech. They continued making furtive glances back to the bar.

Wilhite said, "Things were finally getting too hot for him and his gang. We even had a federal marshal nosing around."

"How did it happen?"

Wilhite allowed his voice to rise to its normal level. "Ambushed, they say. About three weeks ago. I remember the day 'cause we were celebrating. They shipped the last of the Apaches off to Florida. Good riddance, I say."

"Who did it?"

"Don't nobody rightly know for sure, but I suspect some of them Apaches that didn't make it to the train station."

"Then how...."

"Daggart and Henry, they found him north of town a few miles. Buried him on the spot they said."

"Where can I find these men?"

"Oh, hell, Mister Bock, you don't want nothing to do with those two. They're killers, part of Henderson's old gang."

"You say Tule Henderson's dead. Everybody in town says he's dead, but nobody except those two saw his body. I have to know."

"For God's sakes why? Tule's gone. Enjoy it like the rest of us."

"Where are they?"

"Gone. With Tule out of the picture, that gang of his just broke up, scattered. Last I heard Henry's crawled into a bottle and ain't come out since Tule left. He always was a drunkard.

"Where's this Henry now?"

"Oh, hell, Mister Bock, you don't want nothing to do with that man. If he don't shoot you in the back, the smell alone will kill you."

Brodie balled his fist as if he was holding his emotions in a tight grip. "I just want to talk to him."

"Just walk around town, the back of town I mean. Look for a miserable dung heap wearing an old derby with a feather in it.

"Thanks, Mister Wilhite."

"You must have some powerful need to chase after a dead man."

"What about Daggart?"

"Nobody's seen him in weeks. He disappeared right after. Henry, he'll know."

Brodie placed several coins on the bar. "I'll take a bottle of that James Pepper with me."

"Oh, hell, Mister Bock, you can do better 'n that swill."

"It's not for me."

Wilhite took the coins. He handed over a bottle of whiskey. "I see where you're going with this, Mister Bock. You watch your back."

"Sure thing."

"And hold your nose."
Brodie took the bottle and walked out the door.

36

Brodie put the bottle in his saddle bags and rode along the railroad tracks that paralleled First Street until he arrived at a livery stable where he made arrangements for bedding down his horse for the night. He borrowed a small canvas sack for the bottle of whisky and walked out into the golden glow of a desert sundown. Frosty's Café provided a decent meal and enough time to plan out the rest of the evening. When he left the café, the sky to the west was a deep blue, but above the stars sparkled in a black sky.

A waiter at Frosty's provided directions to the seedier side of town and he was about to turn off the main street for that area when a large man approached, a man with a badge.

"Evening, Mister."

"Evening, Marshal."

"New in town?"

"Yes, Sir. Just passing through."

"My name's Jessup. And you're...."

"Bock."

"I thought so. You're looking for Tule Henderson I hear."

"How...."

"It's part of my job, son. Wilhite told me.

"I'm not looking for trouble, if that's what you're hinting at."

"I'm not hinting at all, son. Tule Henderson's dead."

"That's the rumor, I hear."

"Fact or fiction, Tule ain't here."

"Do you think he's still alive, that he faked his death?"

"It don't rightly matter, son. He's gone from these parts and that's that."

"Some might see it that way."

"Then I take it your business here is about done?

"Come first light, I'll be gone."

"Enjoy your stay in Lordsburg, Mister Bock." Jessup tipped his hat, a move that seemed genuine, and walked away.

I have to act fast. He turned from the well-lit streets and entered the darker regions of town. Brodie took his time, looking for a derby hat with a feather on each man he encountered. A swirling wind brought the smell of strong disinfectant, a sign as obvious as a red lantern over a door for those familiar with a town's cribs. He was at the edge of town where a series of small hovels reeking of that smell, of alcohol and worse were the homes and workplaces of the whores who had finally reached bottom. The only things life offered after the cribs was suicide, murder or a slow and painful death by any number of foul diseases.

Brodie shuddered and entered the ally. He walked slowly and pretended to stumble along like a drunk. Moaning voices sneaked from some of the cribs – some in false passion, some in anger and some just in pain. He walked up and down the filthy street for some time before he saw Henry. The man in the derby with the feather fell backwards out of a crib and into the street. He wore longjohns that looked filthy even in the faint light coming from inside the crib. His pants were down to his knees and he had to brace himself against the adobe wall to struggle into a standing position. He pulled up his pants, pulled the suspenders over his shoulders and grabbed a small knife from one of the pockets.

"I'm gonna cut you!"

Brodie ran to the crib and arrived seconds after Henry stumbled back in. The drunk held the woman by her neck as he raised the knife above her head. Brodie stepped in and grabbed the man's arm, pulling him back from the stinking bed. Henry fell to the ground and the knife slid into the street. The woman worked her way across the rubber-sheet bed covering and into the corner of the room. Even in the dim light from her lantern he could see she was covered in bruises. Her face reflected terror.

Brodie forced a friendly voice. "What's the trouble here, Henry?"

"I'm gonna cut that bitch. Who the hell are you?"

"Oh, hell, partner, you know me. Let's get out of here."

"I'm gonna kill 'at bitch."

"She ain't worth it. Besides, Jessup's on the prowl."

"He don't scare me."

"I got us a bottle."

"Huh?"

"Whiskey. Let's kill that instead of her."

Henry stepped back, stumbled and fell, and crawled out of the crib on all fours. Again he used the exterior wall as a brace to stand up. "C'mon."

Brodie took a few coins from his pocket and dropped them on the table by the lantern. "Get yourself some doctoring, Ma'am."

She said nothing, but her liver-spotted right hand grabbed the coins.

Brodie stepped outside. "Come on, Henry. Let's go do some serious drinking." He opened the canvas sack and showed off the bottle of cheap whiskey.

Henry grinned. "Where do I know you from?"

"Hell."

Henry stopped and nearly fell over. "Where's that?"

Brodie pulled out the bottle, pulled out the cork and took a drink. "Do you want to talk or do you want to drink?" He handed the bottle over. Henry grabbed it as if it was a lifeline. He put the bottle to his lips and swallowed twice.

Brodie took it back and put the cork back in. "Let's go."

"Where we going?"

"Let's find someplace quiet where we can catch up on old times. Some place where you're downwind." Henry didn't seem to notice the insult. He stumbled on.

Brodie led him east past the edge of town and then north to the railroad tracks. They paused so Henry could take another swallow. Brodie took the bottle back, but didn't drink. They walked at least a half a mile out of town before Brodie sat down on the tracks and gestured for Henry to follow. The drunk tried to sit down with some feigned dignity, but only succeeded in falling on his butt. Brodie handed him the bottle. Henry drank some more and handed it back.

Far, far in the distant east a train horn sounded. It was a long, lonely wail that teased at the edge of awareness.

Henry said, "We know each other?"

"We've met."

"Where? You don't look all that familiar." Henry slurred and he had to force some of the words.

"Utah. Medicine Hat."

"I been there."

Brodie handed over the bottle again. "You surely have. Drink up, my friend."

"I still don't remember you none."

Brodie began unbuttoning his shirt. "I never thought I'd live to see you again, Henry." He pulled down the shirt and pointed to a scar on his chest, the scar from an old bullet wound. See that?"

"Too damn dark."

Henry blinked and fell over onto the tracks. Brodie pulled his shirt back on. He reached over and pulled Henry up. He slapped him in the face several times. "Come out of it."

"Wha…."

"Where's Tule Henderson?"

"Dead."

"You found him? Buried him?"

"Didn't bury him none."

"Is he dead?"

"Who?"

"Daggart, then. Where the hell is he?"

"He's not dead, like Tule. Nobody's dead like Tule." Henry nodded off.

"Damn you." Brodie slapped him back to consciousness.

"Where's Daggart?"

"Purchase."

"Are you certain?"

"Yeah. Where's that bottle?"

Brodie handed over the bottle again. About a third of the whiskey was left. "Kill it."

Henry laughed, slobbering. "Don't mind if I do."

"You're sure about Purchase?"

"Sure as shootin,' Mister." He finished the whiskey and fell back unconscious between the tracks. The bottle shattered against one of the rails. Brodie stood up. The train moving in from the east wailed again. He could see the faint light approaching in the distance. Brodie stepped off the tracks and looked down on Henry.

"When you shoot a man, you'd better kill a man."

Brodie walked away quickly and made his way to the livery stable. As the train raced through town, Brodie rode out and headed west toward Purchase, Arizona Territory.

37

He rode almost due west through a vast plain with mountains to the north and south. The desert was flat, broken only by washes and scrub brush. When Lordsburg was several hours behind, he stopped to grab as much sleep as possible before sunrise. As he slept, rapidly moving clouds replaced the stars. The wind picked up and a clap of thunder in the distance woke him.

"Oh, hell."

A dark wall of blowing sand reaching hundreds of feet in the air moved swiftly toward him. Behind it lightning blasted light through the darkness and thunder rattled the earth. Brodie grabbed his saddle and was putting it on the horse when the wall of sand slammed into them. The animal spooked and reared up. The saddle slid off and knocked Brodie to the ground and as he jumped up to grab the reins. The horse bolted and ran into the night.

Brodie shouldered his saddle and followed as the sand turned to a hard rain. Lightning bright enough to show the colors of the desert exploded all around and the air around him rumbled with each blast of thunder. Lightning flashes allowed him to follow the hoof prints of his horse for a few moments, but the rain soon erased them. It fell hard and heavy, like buck shot splashing in a pool of muddy water. He walked in the direction of the last set of tracks.

Sunrise found Brodie plodding through mud six inches to a foot or more deep. The flat desert sand was a snare, the muck pulling at each footstep. Invisible hands seemed to grab each boot every time he raised his feet from the earth. The humidity rose as did the sun and the heat and each step became a challenge to his physical strength and his will to go on. At mid-morning he saw something out of the ordinary to his west, something that just didn't seem right. Shimmering heat waves and the distance made the object difficult to see. *What the hell?* He plodded on in that direction. Within minutes he recognized his horse – bogged down.

He moved as quickly as he could, but getting to the horse took a lot of time and energy. He was exhausted when he reached the animal – exhausted and quickly heartbroken. The animal had stumbled in the mud and had broken its right leg. All it's fumbling around after the storm had made the situation, the damage, and the pain much worse. Brodie wasted no time. He pulled out his revolver and freed the animal from its fear and agony.

Me next?

Brodie stepped out and struggled on toward higher ground to the west. Thirst wasn't a problem. Each time he pulled a boot from the muck the depression filled with water. To drink, he soaked his shirt in the water and then squeezed the fluid into his mouth. The process filtered most of the sand while providing several moments of respite from the struggle. As the sun crossed overhead the air became thick, almost steaming. Late in the day he noticed that the depth of his footsteps became more and more shallow. By the time the sun set, he was walking on solid ground and approaching the foothills of the Chiricahua Mountains. He turned northwest to seek the road leading to Apache Pass and Fort Bowie.

He spent the night curled up against his saddle. Completely exhausted, he slept from just after sundown until the sunrise slapped him in the face. Without pause, Brodie stood up, grabbed his saddle and started walking. *Keep moving. Just keep moving.*

He reached the road running east to west about noon. His sole purpose in life at that moment was to put one foot in front of the other, take a step, and then repeat the process. Hours later he stumbled and fell onto the side of the road. He struggled to stand back up, struggled and failed. Brodie looked to the northwest, toward Utah and Mexican Hat. "Enid, I…." He fell back against his saddle and stared at the road.

The unmistakable sound of a horse-drawn wagon blew in on a slight breeze from the east. He looked up and followed its progress until the driver slowed down and halted. The freight wagon was painted black and the edges were trimmed in gold paint. Someone had painted a crude-but-colorful desert flower on each side. Small brass and glass candle holders were mounted on each of the four corners. Brodie stared at a death coach.

The driver, a portly man with a friendly face said, "You look like you could use a ride, Mister. Throw your saddle in the back and hop up here for some conversation."

Brodie shook his head as if to shake out the image.

The driver grinned. "Don't worry, mister. We ain't totin' anybody just yet." He pulled the brake and hopped down. "You look like you could use a hand." He took the saddle and tossed it into the empty bed of the hearse. Brodie climbed into the seat. The driver joined him, reached under the seat and handed over a canteen. Brodie took a few swallows and handed it back.

"Thanks. My name's Bock."

"Lord Peter Wiggam." He winked. "I added the 'Lord' because my ma, fussing at me like she done, always said 'Lord, Peter Wiggam,' you are a mess... Lord, Peter Wiggam, what have you gone and done now....'" His laugh filled the desert. "I'm headed to Purchase. You want me to drop you off at Fort Bowie, Mister Bock."

"Purchase sounds just fine to me, if you don't mind."

"Not a bit. 'preciate the company, Mr. Bock."

"And it's Bock, just Bock."

"Call me Lord Peter. Are you a drinking man, Bock-Just-Bock?"

"I've been known to—"

"Say no more." Wiggam produced a bottle of halfway decent whiskey.

They were not quite drunk when they made it through Apache Pass. Wiggam ignored the pathway to the Fort and continued down the road. He pointed up a nearby hill. "That's where it all started. I was here then, a private."

"It?"

"Twenty years of torture and killin'. The Apache wars. If you ask me, it all started right there. We tried to rope, hog-tie and brand old

Cochise up there. Lied to the old boy, they did. But that rascal, he wasn't having any of it. You lie to an Apache, Bock-Just-Bock, and you got an enemy. You kill some of his family and you got yourself a war – twenty years of it."

"I never heard that."

"It's not something the gummint wants people reading in the papers."

"Well, there aren't any more Apaches in Arizona."

"There's always gonna be Apaches in Arizona."

The bumpy road and the whiskey kept Wiggam rattling on about his early experiences as a soldier, miner and jack-of-all-trades. Brodie listened and took note of information he might find useful. He enjoyed the ride. And the whiskey. They turned south at a dusty crossroads and headed southwest toward Purchase.

"What the hell are you doing driving this contraption, Lord Peter?"

Wiggam raised his head and laughed. "Funeral coach for hire. Most of these here towns spring up fast and die off just as fast. They don't hardly have time to grow a suitable funeral parlor. But some of 'em still want a fancy sendoff when the time comes."

"I see."

"Yes, Sir. I'm pretty much the only game in town this side of the Dragoons. You get over Tombstone way and I got competition. We tend to stick to our own territory."

"I'd say it's a pretty good living."

"Sending off the dead proper ain't ever going out of business. People are just dyin' to ride in this thing." Again, his laughter filled the desert. For the first time in many, many months, Brodie laughed, too.

38

"Well, that's it, Bock-Just-Bock – Purchase, Arizona Territory, your basic boom waiting to go bust."

"Hell, man, it looks like an armed camp."

Except for the unusual number of armed citizens, Purchase looked like a hundred other boom towns. Canvas tents had given away to wooden walls with canvas tops. A few wooden buildings had already been constructed. The planks and posts had surely been torn down from the most recent boom and bust town down the road or on the other side of the hill. It was the way of things in the West. Use it, tear it down, move it down the road and reuse it at the next big strike. Reuse and recreate. The same could be said for many of the men and women who followed the treasure mountains.

"What was your name in the states?"

"Smith."

"Yeah, me too."

Brodie studied the scene. Purchase had one main street and it was a busy one. The sound of mining in the nearby rocky hills provided a constant, just audible background rumble, broken only by the occasional explosion of dynamite down in the catacombs. Ore wagons creaked and groaned on their way out of town to the nearest mill, kicking up a thin haze of rock dust in the sunlight. The miners in town running errands, coming on or off their shifts, or just heading into one of the four saloons were armed with rifles or shotguns. A few wore side arms.

"This is downright peculiar," Brodie said.

"Where can I drop you off, Bock-Just-Bock?"

"Anywhere I can find work."

Wiggam looked up and down the street. "Stick with me a bit. I suspect I'll be in a position to offer you some day-work."

"Grave digging?"

"Hell, no. Riding shotgun."

Wiggam drove the wagon through town, stopping in front of the Townsend Mine and Milling Company building, a single story structure with a large window facing the street. "You wait here while I see what's what." He hopped off the wagon and walked inside the building. Brodie stepped down and stretched. He walked around, stretched some more, and took a good look at the town. Everything was new and at the same time showing signs of old age – remnants of previous use.

Wiggam stepped out of the building. "I got work for you if you're interested."

"I'm interested."

"The pay ain't much, but it'll get you a meal, a couple of drinks and maybe even a bath."

"What's the job?"

"Like I figured – riding shotgun."

"For a funeral?"

"C'mon, I'll fill you in."

They climbed on the wagon and Wiggam drove to the end of town, turned around and drove along the backside of the town's structures, pulling up at the rear entrance to the Townsend building. Wiggam said, "You stay here. Keep your eyes busy. And be ready to put that sidearm of yours to work."

"Who am I going to be shooting at?"

"Later." Wiggam jumped down and walked quickly to the back door. It opened before he could knock. Two men struggled with a narrow, wooden coffin made of old planks. They brought it out and loaded it into the hearse. Wiggam watched their movements, but he also scanned the tops of the nearby hills. The two Townsend workers picked up a couple of shovels leaning against the back of the building and hopped into the back of the wagon. Wiggam jumped back into the seat and started the wagon back toward the edge of town.

"Where are we going," Brodie said.

"Graveyard."

"I got that part figured out."

"Up that little hill." He jerked his head to the right.

The road out of town forked and Wiggam turned uphill and to the right. Several crude wooden crosses and piles of earth and stones marked their destination.

"It's a might busy for such a new town," Brodie said.

Two more men, armed, waited. They held shovels. When the wagon reached the top of the hill, Brodie noticed three freshly dug graves. When he stopped, the waiting men joined the two in the back of the wagon in lifting the coffin out. They carried it to the edge of the first grave and began to make preparations for the burial.

Wiggam said, "Come on, Bock-Just-Bock. We got two more to go." He turned to the men by the grave and addressed the two who had come up with them. "You gents coming?"

"Just a minute, you old fart." They finished placing the ropes for lowering the coffin and then walked swiftly back to the wagon. They jumped on as Wiggam pulled out.

They brought the other two coffins up one at a time. A well-dressed man accompanied them on the last trip. He rode a beautiful horse and sat on an expensive saddle. He dismounted at the head of the graves and tied the reins to a nearby wooden cross. He walked by the graves and examined each one with care. "All right, men."

The four men from town lowered the coffins into the graves. Afterwards, they stood in formation around them as the mine owner said a few words. One of the men crossed himself. Townsend nodded and they began filling in the graves. Townsend walked over to Wiggam and Brodie. "It's not much, but these were good men and they deserved a final ride with some class. The men, the others I mean, the miners and all, will… well, this hearse of yours will mean more than you can know."

Brodie said, "I noticed nobody showed up for the services."

"Purchase is a town for mining, not mourning."

He handed Wiggam an envelope.

Wiggam said, "Thank you, Mr. Townsend. Sir, I'd like you to meet… Bock is his name. That's all I can get out of him. He'll make a good hand if you know somebody looking for a hard worker."

"I just might." He stuck out his hand. "July Townsend."

Brodie shook his hand. "Pleased to meet you."

"You have a firm grip, Mr. Bock… I mean, Bock. Are you seeking employment?"

"Yes, Sir, I am."

"What can you do?"

"Well, I can ride. I grew up on a ranch. I can work the dumbass end of a sledge hammer. I can follow orders and I'm no shirker."

"Can you handle yourself around a rifle? A pistol?"

"I've been known to win a few shooting contests."

"Yes, but shooting a target isn't the same as shooting a man."

"I've had some experience at that, too, sir."

Townsend's eyes narrowed.

Brodie spoke quickly. "Never on the wrong side of the law, Mr. Townsend."

"Well, let's see what kind of shot you are, Bock." He turned to Wiggam. "Let's ride out of town a ways. I'll buy a few rounds at the Cavalier to pay for your time."

Wiggam smiled. "I've worked harder for a lot less. It's a deal."

Townsend tied his horse to the back of the wagon and climbed on-to the seat. Brodie climbed in the back and sat down behind. "Ride on down the road south of town about a mile or so."

Townsend motioned to stop at the edge of a wash where it curved near the road. Brodie and Wiggam followed when Townsend stepped down. He pointed to a large root curving in and out halfway up the wash, about 25 yards distant. "How close can you come to hitting that root, Bock?"

Brodie took only a few seconds to aim before firing five shots. Each one struck the root.

"Not bad," Townsend said.

Brodie reloaded.

"How are you with moving targets?" Townsend pointed to a chip-munk scurrying from scrub to scrub.

Brodie aimed and fired. The shot kicked up sand in front of the small animal. It quickly turned around and ran back. Brodie fired and again a blast of sand forced the creature to turn. It dashed across the sand and into a hole beneath a small scrub brush. Brodie fired three more times and three thin limbs fell to the earth. "I don't kill for sport, Mr. Townsend."

"You're hired, Bock."

"He'll make you a good hand, Mr. Townsend."

"Just what kind of hand will I be," Brodie said.

Townsend's demeanor changed. His voice was cold and steady, "Well, you won't be killing for sport."

"This work, it's on the right side of the law?"

"I am the law, Bock. But you won't be told to do anything your conscience can't bear."

"I'll take the job, sir, at least until I can get on my feet again."

Townsend led them back to the wagon. "I keep a room over the Cavalier for guests and such. It's noisy as hell, but the bed's solid and you can eat on the mine's tab for a day or so – until you get settled in."

"Thank you."

As Brodie and Wiggam climbed back into the wagon, Townsend mounted his horse. "Meet me at the Cavalier, gentlemen." He rode off and was halfway back to town before Wiggam had the wagon turned around.

Wiggam said, "Well, sir, it looks like you're sitting in high cotton."

"I need a stake. This will do."

"This here job of yours might do more than that."

"Meaning?"

"In that office of his, Townsend's got one of them chalk boards – the kind you see in some schools. It's got a list of jobs and some names on it."

"Like I said, meaning?"

"Meaning one of them names is Daggart."

39

Townsend waved them to the back of the saloon where he sat at a table like a baron. He poured three shot glasses full of a very good brand of whiskey. He raised his glass and his guests followed his example. "Three shots in honor of three good men."

Brodie said, "Who were they?"

"Hell, I don't know their names."

"Smith," Wiggam said.

Townsend laughed. "To Smith, each one of 'em."

Townsend poured again and the three men sat back and relaxed. No one spoke for a moment until Townsend said, "Go ahead, Bock, ask the question that's on your mind."

"This work you're hiring me for… I am no gunman."

"I don't need, nor do I want, gunmen. The Townsend Number One needs guards, guards who can hit what they shoot and who are damn careful about who they shoot."

"I don't get you, Mr. Townsend."

"Bock, can you shoot in the dark?"

"Any damn fool can shoot in the dark."

"Let's say semi-darkness, by candlelight."

"If I can see it, I can hit it."

Wiggam reached for the bottle. He paused a second, until Townsend nodded his head. Wiggam refreshed his drink and topped off Brodie's glass. "I got an idea where this here conversation is going."

Townsend nodded his head when offered a refill. "We have an interesting situation, gentlemen. And a dangerous one. Townsend Number One cuts into that big ridge out there from the east side. We hit a big vein, one that could last years."

Brodie nodded.

Wiggam said, "I sense one of them 'oh, buts' coming."

Townsend nodded. "Weasel Hunter and his men moved over on the west side and started tunneling in. They hit the same vein."

Wiggam said, "East is east 'n west is west but them twains has done met, eh?"

"Meet, hell. They slammed into each other. Hunter has a camp on the other side – calls it a town. Hunterville." Townsend spat on the floor and poured another drink.

Wiggam reached out. "Don't mind if I do."

Brodie shook his head. "That explains the hardware."

"So far the fighting's been fist and club... but it's going to get worse. When it does, I need a man down there who can think as well as shoot."

"When do I start, Mr. Townsend?"

"Grab some breakfast at first light and then come on over to the office. I'll escort you up there and get you started."

Later, Brodie escorted Wiggam to his rig. "You're moving on, I take it?"

"I got business over in Pearce, but I'll be back through in a few days." He looked down the street and then up to the cemetery. "I got a feeling there's gonna be more work here real soon."

"You take care, Wiggam."

"You, too, Bock-Just-Bock. I'd like to see you riding my wagon from the front; not as a passenger."

Wiggam rode out of town. After he crested the nearby hills and was out of sight, Brodie turned and walked down the street.

The entrance to Townsend Number One was a small A-frame about the size of the entrance to an average saloon. Instead of batwings, the entrant stepped through a near-constant cloud of dust punctuated by the smell of too many men working without benefit of a bath. Each miner carried either a pistol or large knife and their somewhat awkward gait proved they were unused to carrying such tools at work. Townsend's number two man, Stove Upmann, led the way. Brodie stepped through and entered a large dome of hewn rock. Several tunnels led into different directions, most of them ending a short distance from their entrance. Another and larger tunnel led down a steep incline.

Upmann said, "Your station will be up near the entrance, but you'll need to know your way around in case you hear the call." He picked up two felt hats from a stack on a nearby shelf. Each had a forward brim and a Z-shaped metal plate affixed to the front. The plates held small picks holding candles. He lit each candle from a candle on a holder rammed into the wall and handed a hat to Brodie.

"Thanks. What exactly am I supposed to do when I get that call, Stove?"

"Damn, it, you call me Mister Upmann. Or Upmann. Or just hey boss, but don't you dare used that other... thing."

"Sure thing, Mister Upmann."

"Hell, make it Upmann." He gestured and Brodie followed him down the narrow tunnel. They descended a hundred feet or so until the tunnel opened into another large vault. A few small prospects had been probed into the wall around the vault, but only one main tunnel, a straight horizontal shaft, was in operation. Brodie waited until an ore cart passed by and then leaned over to examine the darkness. He could make out shapes of men working – dark shadows barely illuminated by burning candles jammed into the rock or worn on their caps.

"Good men. They're why you're here," Upmann said.

"About my job and that call you mentioned...."

A gunshot exploded at the far end of the tunnel, the bullet ricocheting several times off the walls. Men shouted as the lights along the tunnel walls darkened. The lights from the candles on the miner's caps darkened at the same time, some in motion like falling stars as the men jumped to the floor of the mine. Brodie and Upmann instantly backed from the tunnel on each side of the entrance. Several more shots rattled the walls.

"It's started," Upmann said.

"What's started?"

"Your new job, that's what. Protect these men."

"How the hell can I do that?"

Several miners scrambled out and scattered around the vault.

Upmann shouted, "How many back in there."

One of the miners sat up. He was pale and shaking, but his face showed anger. "Five more." He looked to Brodie. "Who's he?"

"Payback."

The miner smiled.

Another man crawled out of the tunnel. He hopped up and joined the others. Upmann helped pull another man through. "All of you out of here. A ricochet can kill just as fast as a direct hit."

The men scurried up the tunnel. Three more men scrambled out of the tunnel. They were breathing heavily. Upmann helped pull them out and shove them on their way. "That's four. Who's left?"

The miners had wasted no time in making for the tunnel to the top of the mine. One turned. "Daggart."

Brodie said, "Was he hit?"

"I don't know. I think so. Maybe. He's still back in there; that's all I know."

A voice shouted from the far end of the tunnel. "Hey, you Townsend men. Come on back for some more, you sumbitches!" A single shot followed and more laughter followed the shot. "Come and get it."

Upmann, sat back, resigned. "Go on, we'll be right behind you. The miner jogged up the tunnel. "It looks like things heated up sooner 'n I figured. This is why Townsend hired you. We have to protect these men."

"And your gold."

"Gold ain't nothin' without the men to dig it, Brodie."

"What about Daggart?"

"What about him?"

"You can't leave a man behind."

"If ever there was a man I could leave behind...."

The voice from the far end of the tunnel interrupted. "Hey, Townsend. Hey, we done got one 'o your boys. I hear 'im moanin' for his mamma."

"He's alive," Brodie said.

"Maybe. They might just be trying to get a few of us up into the shooting gallery."

"And maybe you got an injured man in your mine."

"Daggart ... damn."

"You need me in there, Upmann."

"I'll round up a few men first."

"Hell, they're no good; not for this kind of work."

"These miners are some—"

"Half a dozen men came out of that hole and they were all armed. How many of 'em fired back?"

Upmann forced a sad grin. "I see your point. Do you think you can really get in there without getting yourself killed?"

Brodie pinched the wick on his candle. He nodded and Upmann did the same. Brodie eased down flat on the mine's floor. "You shout and fire a few rounds down there. Aim for the end of the tunnel so you don't hit Daggart."

"I ain't totally stupid, Brodie."

"I'll crawl in and start making my way up the tunnel. I'll get to Daggart and go from there."

Upmann stood up and walked around the vault pinching out the candles. Soon the room was illuminated by the faint light of candles in the exit tunnel. He leaned around the entrance to the main tunnel and pulled his pistol. He aimed for the distant and faint light that marked the break where the Townsend and Hunter mines met. Upmann fired four shots slowly. Brodie crawled in the entrance and was soon in darkness.

40

Brodie crawled slowly along the rough rock. Remaining unseen was easy in the darkness. Remaining unheard was a significant challenge. The floor of the tunnel was covered with loose rock that crunched or rolled, betraying movement. Fleeing miners had dropped their tools, so metal and wood noisemakers also littered the floor. He felt the floor with his hands and gently shoved aside any obstruction that could betray his location. His progress was slow.

A shot echoed through the tunnel. The bullet hit near the place where the competing mines met.

Shooting at Daggart, Brodie thought.

He used the echo and the laughter following the shot to move quickly and when the noise died, he had edged several yards closer to his goal. Movement at the junction of the tunnels caused him to stop as a yellow-gold, soft light lit up the darkness. A kerosene lantern tied to the end of a long pole seemed to float through the tunnel.

A miner with a cruel twist to his voice said, "We got you, boy. Why don't you come on and show yourself." The glow moved slowly into the tunnel. The man holding the pole was hidden by the rock wall.

A dark movement behind a pile of rubble caught Brodie's attention. *Daggart!* He hugged the floor, but continued to move forward. Brodie and the glow from the lantern moved toward Daggart at about the same speed.

The unseen miner spoke again. "We comin' for you, boy."

Brodie pulled his pistol, aimed and fired. The lantern blew up in a blast of light. It and the pole that had carried it fell to ground. Brodie used the momentary excitement to crawl next to Daggart. Each man was protected from the other tunnel by a pile of fresh rubble, which provided a small wall between the factions.

Brodie spoke softly. "Daggart?"

"Yeah."

"Name's Bock. I came to get you."

"About damn time."

"Are you hurt?"

"They got me in the leg. The bone's shattered and I'm bleeding like a stuck pig."

Brodie felt the man's leg. Daggart screamed when Brodie felt the jagged bone protruding though the muscle of the man's right thigh. Blood pooled beneath the wound.

Daggart's voice was weak. "I'm bleeding to death. You gotta get me out of here, Bock."

The miner from the other end of the tunnel shouted. "Ya' missed me, sumbitch." Several wild shots followed. They ricocheted off the walls, but did no damage. "We'll be comin' for you soon, boy. Soon."

Daggart's voice showed panic. "They're going to rush us."

"Well, this is where I leave you."

Daggart grabbed Brodie's arm. His grip was desperate, but weak. "You can't leave me."

"I'm not taking on a bunch of miners just to save your ass." He made out as if he was about to crawl away.

"Gold, Bock. It's high-grade and it's all yours. Don't let me die like this."

Brodie paused as if thinking over the proposition. He leaned closer. "I don't want your gold Daggart."

"Anything!"

"Where's Tule Henderson?"

Daggart choked. "Dead."

"Sure. Good luck with Hunter's men." He crawled back.

"Wait! Bock, wait!" Daggart's voice was a whisper.

"I'm waiting."

"You're him ain't you? The one's been huntin' Tule all these years."

"Where is he?"

"I don't know."

"Bye. You enjoy what's coming, Daggart."

"He's alive. We done faked the killin' and...." He passed out.

Brodie slapped him back into consciousness. "Where is he?"

"Jesse... Jesse Cross... knows...." He passed out again.

Footsteps of several men echoed down the tunnel from the Hunter side. Brodie slapped Daggart again. "Where's Cross? Where!"

"Don't leave me."

"Where!"

"Tableau... Jesse knows...."

When Brodie crawled back he pushed against Daggart's shattered leg. The man screamed and then fainted. As Brodie crawled away, the blood flow from Daggart's wound pulsed slowly, slower and then stopped.

Brodie took a chance by standing up and running out of the tunnel. When he entered the vault, Upmann waited. Brodie shook his head. "Dead."

"He wasn't much of a man, but damn. And this is just getting started."

"Upmann, do you want to end this fight right now?"

Upmann looked at the blood on Brodie's hands. "How?"

"There's a good many of Hunter's men in that tunnel, riled up and smelling blood. I think they're going to rush your end of this hole."

Upmann stood up straight. "By God, we'll be ready."

"No, sir. Let 'em come on in. The more the better."

"I don't understand."

"Rats in a trap. Let 'em come on in. Egg 'em on. Once they're in here... hell, a kid with a slingshot could hold the entrance. They're bottled up. You and your men rush over this hill and plug up the other end. Game over."

Upmann leaned against the wall. His fingers rapidly tapped the rock.

Brodie said, "You don't have much time."

Upmann moved to the incline. "Come on."

A moment later Brodie and Upmann faced the assembled miners. Upmann spoke. "Daggart's dead."

"Good riddance."

Several miners nodded and mumbled in agreement. Upmann raised his arms. "The kind of man he was don't matter. What does matter is that Daggart was a miner – one of us. You know what kind of men are on the other side of that hill. And you know Daggart's just the first. Unless we do something about it." He grabbed Brodie by the arm and moved him forward. "This man here, Bock, has an idea."

Brodie took another step closer to the miners. "Hunter's men are moving into the mine. They're going to come through and take it."

"Like hell!"

"Let 'em come!"

Brodie raised his voice. "That's right. Let 'em come. Only we won't be here. You men are armed. You're ready for a fight, but are you ready to put an end to this? Right now?"

"Hell, yes!"

Brodie continued. "While they're pouring into the mine, we'll sneak over the ridge and catch them from behind." He looked over to the foreman.

Upmann stepped up beside him. "Mr. Townsend hired you for this. It's your show."

Brodie pointed to the miners. "We have to move fast, men. Split up right down the middle." He pointed to the men on his left. "You men scramble up the ridge to the north. When these other men do the same on the south, rush the tunnel from both ends. Most of their gunmen will be trapped in or near the mine."

A miner stepped forward. "How can we be sure?"

"Because I'll be down there making sure they do."

Upmann said, "I'll go with you."

"These are your men and they need you with them. I'll go it alone down there."

"Are you sure?"

"We need to make an end of this."

"When do we move?"

"Now. Get on over that ridge."

Upmann pointed to one of the miners. "Earl, you lead the north side group. Whoever gets to the ridge line first waits until the others catch up. We rush 'em all at once, all together."

Earl led his group away. Upmann looked to Brodie, but before he could speak, Brodie held up his pistol. "I can take care of myself down there, Upmann. You just take care of the other end."

Upmann nodded and his men moved toward the hill. Brodie grabbed the man's arm. "Do you know a Jesse Cross?"

"Sure, who doesn't?"

"Where can I find him?"

"Can this wait?"

"I need to know, Upmann."

"Well, first—"

Shouts from his men cut short the sentence. "Later. I got to go." Upmann joined his men and led them around the mine's exterior and up the hill. Earl's group was already a quarter of the way up the ridge. Brodie looked to his horse, shook his head and stepped back into the mine. He eased quietly down the incline to the main vault. He heard men's voices, near whispers, from the far end of the main shaft. Hunter's men were making their move to take the Townsend Number One. They were unfamiliar with the tunnel and its potential dangers, so the man in the lead had lit a candle. He held it out from his body. The faint glow revealed at least half a dozen shadowy figures behind. Brodie was in near darkness. The only light was a faint glow from the exterior sunlight striking the incline's walls behind him.

Brodie shouted, "Far enough!"

"We jes' getting' started, boy."

Someone, probably the man doing the shouting, fired two shots down the tunnel. One of the bullet ricocheted up the incline. The other struck one of the wooden support beams. Brodie dropped to the ground, rolled to the entrance of the tunnel and fired three shots. Shouts and a couple of screams followed. As Brodie rolled away from the entrance several more shots smacked into the walls of the vault.

"You done in now, boy. We comin' for you."

"Come and get it!" Brodie rolled into the entrance again and fired three more shots – one to the left, one centered and one to the right. Another man screamed. Brodie rolled away as more shots hit the vault walls.

He heard several voices, but the words were spoken quietly and he could not make out what was being said. Another shot echoed through the tunnel followed by silence and then more muffled voices. A moment later Brodie heard what sounded like men dragging something away. He could also make out a faint moaning from two different voices.

They're leaving. He reloaded his pistol and then rolled slowly and carefully into the entrance of the tunnel. He could see nothing in the darkness, but the sounds of men retreating were obvious. He crawled in and followed. This time Brodie moved even more slowly and more carefully than before, his hearing alert for the faintest sound of someone left behind for an ambush. His hand touched a pool of warm blood – Daggart's blood.

Lie down with dogs....

Brodie wiped his hand and eased forward. He heard nothing except the voices, which got louder as they approached the far end of the tunnel. The miners had stopped well inside the tunnel and were examining their wounded.

"Hell, they got *three* of us."

"And we probably hit some of them."

"Maybe."

"I only heard one pistol. I think there's only one man in there, some kind of rear guard."

"Let's get down there and get this over with."

"Damn straight."

"We're sitting ducks in there."

"I got me an idea. Drag these boys out and bring that little table out there back in here."

The voices came from harshly backlit figures huddled near the mine entrance. Three men dragged three wounded men away. When they returned they carried a small, rectangular wooden table. Upended it would make a perfect shield for moving down the mine tunnel.

The leader of the group spoke. "Two inch think planks, boys. Ain't no bullet goin' through that. We'll work our way down to the vault, spread out and kill every one of them sons of bitches."

"They're miners."

"Sittin' on our mine. This thing ends today."

Most of the men voiced agreement.

Three of the men began to raise the table. Brodie aimed at the shadows and fired three shots. One blew the side of a miner's head off. The second struck the center chest of another miner. The third winged a man in the shoulder. The table fell as the men dropped for cover.

Brodie fired two more shots into the shadows. Another man screamed. Brodie reloaded. When he looked back up the miners were rushing toward their entrance. He moved quickly to follow. The three men he had hit were dead or dying. The others were near the entrance when they stopped. Outside men were shouting. Gunfire exploded from all directions. One of the miners looked out.

"Townsend men!"

The miner had exposed his position to see what was going on. Brodie's next shot struck him in the center of his back.

Brodie shouted to a fictitious army. "Let's get 'em, men!" He fired four more shots, reloaded and moved on. When he reached the entrance he looked out on chaos. Hunterville consisted of only three structures: a small office, what appeared to be a bunkhouse, and a cook shed. Upmann and his men were at the bunkhouse, firing into the office. Several bodies were scattered between the two buildings. Earl and his men were firing into the office. Flying bits of wood spit out by shells smacking into the planks floated on the air like dust. The cookhouse was on fire. Upmann fell. One of his men helped him up. He grasped his shoulder, bloodied, and moved on.

The miners who had run from the tunnel turned and retreated. The first one to near the entrance saw Brodie. He stopped and raised his arms. A shot from one of Earl's men blew through his neck. The man tumbled to the earth, shook violently for a few seconds and then was still. The other men scattered in all directions. Several ran one way and, seeing Townsend's men, turned and ran the other way only to find themselves facing more Townsend guns.

Someone inside the office stuck a white handkerchief on a broom handle out the window. Upmann shouted for his men to cease firing. Several more shots were fired and another of Hunter's men fell before order was established. Hunter's men stopped moving, but kept their hands on their weapons.

A voice from inside the office shouted, "Surrender! We surrender! Call off your men."

Upmann stepped close to the office. "Tell your men to drop their guns. Then come on out – hands in the air."

"Do like he says, men."

Hunter's remaining miners dropped their weapons. The man inside the office stepped out, still holding the flag. Two men followed. They were bleeding from superficial wounds.

Upmann said, "It's over Thompson. Where's Hunter?"

Thompson grinned sourly and pointed to the east. A rider now more than half a mile away left a trail of dust in the air. He was running at full gallop.

Brodie walked through the battleground and stepped close to Upmann. The foreman spoke to Thompson. "Like I said, this is all over. Let's you and me settle it in your office."

"My men?"

"The shootings over. We got a good doc over the hill."

Thompson nodded and stepped back into the office. Upmann started to follow, but Brodie grabbed him by the arm. "Jesse Cross?"

"I got important business, Bock." He shook off Brodie's hand.

"Where's Jesse Cross? I have to know."

Upmann recognized the look in Brodie's eyes, the stare of a mountain lion about to leap. "Hell, Bock, everybody knows Jesse. Just ask." He made half a turn toward the office and paused. "All right?"

"Sure." He relaxed and glanced around at the violent scene. "What next, Upmann?"

"What always happens after a battle. Leaders make deals and soldiers bleed." He finished the turn and entered the office.

Across the small encampment Earl sat on a bench seat next to the bunkhouse. He was wrapping a bandage on his arm. Brodie joined him and helped tie off the bandage. Earl shook his head. "They shouldn't have pushed on through."

"Do you know a Jesse Cross?"

"Sure." Earl looked around slowly. Half a dozen or more Hunter men were in the dirt, never to get up on their own power again. Only one of the Townsend men remained still, a lonely figure draped over a rock on the hillside. Several were tending each other's wounds. The Hunter men sat on their hands next to the office. "It didn't have to happen like this."

"Jesse Cross? Do you know where I can find him?"

Earl turned his head. "Her. Jesse's a woman."

"I need to talk to her."

"If you got ten dollars you got her attention. She's a whore."

"Where?"

"Tableau."

"Where's that?"

"Over near Lordsburg. She runs a house there."

Brodie stood up and walked toward the ridge. He passed several wounded men on his way, but he never slowed down. Within minutes he was over the ridge and out of sight.

He walked slowly downhill toward Purchase. His hands shook slightly and his breathing was rapid. A large diamondback no more than four feet away rattled its warning and raised its head to strike. Brodie stepped away and never slowed down. *Not today. Not today.* He walked directly to Townsend's office where the owner stood and watched him approach.

"What the hell's going on, Bock? I heard shots – lots of 'em."

"You won't have any more trouble from Hunter or his miners, Mr. Townsend. Upmann will give you all the details."

"My men?"

"You lost one. A few wounded."

209

"And Hunter?"

"Riding like hell toward Tombstone. You won't be seeing him soon."

"His men?"

"It's pretty bad. You'll be wanting to make accommodations for those still breathing to move on. I'd find 'em work in Tombstone or Charleston or just about any place else. There's going to be bad blood over this."

Townsend nodded.

"I killed a lot of men, Mr. Townsend."

"Defending lives and property isn't killing, Bock."

"Tell that to the fellows with my bullets in them."

"Yeah."

"I'll be drawing my pay for a day's work now."

"Bock, you just started."

"And the job's over."

The men stared at each other for a moment. Townsend sighed and ushered Brodie into this office. They spoke without saying anything of substance while the mine owner opened a safe and withdrew a small stack of bills. He handed them to Brodie. "You sure you won't stick around?"

Brodie stared at the bills for a moment before putting them in his pocket. "Back home one of my partners talks about the look in a man's eyes when he's seen too much killing. I don't want him to see that in me. I'll be going now."

They shook hands and Brodie left the office and within minutes was riding out of Purchase, retracing his steps across the dry playa, and headed for Tableau and a confrontation with a whore named Jesse Cross.

41

Tableau was a fast-booming town slowly going bust. Just east of Lordsburg, it served the miners and prospectors chiseling a poor living out of the nearby mountains. The slightly more prosperous men who worked to ship the ore from the small mining towns of Steins and Shakespeare earned a larger and somewhat more reliable income. Some ranching money found its way into town, also. Two of the town's original ten buildings had been disassembled and taken away. Three were in ruins and the remaining five were occupied by a general store, a blacksmith shop, two saloons, and The Casa Grande – a whorehouse and the most successful of the remaining businesses.

Brodie rode straight to The Casa Grande. The door was locked and a sign read

Closed

Re-Open 3 p.m.

Jesse

He walked around the building. The back door was locked. When he looked through the windows, each of them, he could see that no one was inside. He walked his horse the short distance to Albino's #1 Saloon.

A short Mexican with a friendly smile beamed when Brodie entered. "Welcome, Senor. I am Albino. How may I serve you?"

"Beer."

"Ah, I have no beer today. I am sorry, Senor. I have some pulque, but I think you would probably prefer whiskey."

"What's pulque?"

"Mexican beer. The old ones call it 'the blood of the goddess.' I don't know what that means, but I am not wise in such things."

Brodie looked around. The only source of information in the saloon was the bartender. "I'll try this pulque of yours."

"Si." Albino grabbed two beer mugs and filled them with a milky white liquid from a near-empty barrel placed under the bar. He shoved the two mugs forward.

"I only ordered one."

"This is one. You drink the first very fast. Very fast."

"Why?"

"To get it over with."

"What the hell." Brodie put the mug to his lips and drained it. He slammed the mug on the bar when finished. "Damnation, Albino. That's awful."

"You want that whiskey now, Senor?"

"Make it fast. Pour a shot for yourself – a reward for trying to warn me."

Albino grinned. "Si. Gracias." He poured two shots. "The other pulque?"

"It's yours."

Albino took the mug in his right hand and held the shot glass in his left. He downed the pulque and followed it immediately with the shot of whiskey.

Brodie killed his whiskey in a single swallow. They looked at each other and laughed.

Brodie said, "Where are the whores, Albino?"

The Mexican's smile vanished. "They are in Lordsburg, Senor. One of the ladies, she died yesterday. They are saying goodbye today."

"Dead? Which one?"

"Her name was Kathleen. Katie they called her. She was a good woman, a schoolteacher, but her husband died in the mines. She had little choice but to...."

"Yeah, I've heard that tale too many times."

"Such a price."

Brodie took the bottle and poured a shot in each glass. He raised his. "To doing what you have to do, my friend."

They touched glasses and killed their drinks.

Albino looked out the door. "Such a terrible price...."

Brodie invested a good part of the afternoon chatting with Albino. The man knew a lot about Tule Henderson who had made the saloon something of a second headquarters. "He favors the lady of the house down the street." Albino winked.

"The one they call Jesse?"

"Very pretty, but with the serpent's sting."

He knew nothing of Henderson's death other than rumor and he refused to speculate on any other possibilities. After another couple of whiskey shots, he leaned over closer to his customer. Although no one else was in the building, he lowered his voice to a near whisper. "Jesse Cross, she will have your answers, Senor."

When they ran out of conversational topics, Brodie moved to a small table in the back of the saloon where he watched the shadows outside deepen. As sundown approached, a man who was well dressed, but dusty, entered and walked straight to the bar. Albino was pouring a double shot of whiskey by the time the man scraped his boot on the wooden rail at the base of the bar. "Well, amigo Albino, we done planted Kate."

"A sad day, my friend."

"Not that you'd know it. Jesse's done open for business like nothin' ever happened."

The two men spoke softly of whores and death for a few moments. Albino left for a moment to relieve himself. When he returned Brodie was gone.

The Casa Grande was lit up, poorly, in the shadows of weak and yellow sundown. Brodie stepped up on the front porch. He rapped the tarnished brass door knocker and within seconds the door opened. A woman of indeterminate age smiled and gestured for him to enter. "C'mon in, stranger. Whatever you need, we got and if we don't got it you sure as hell don't need it." She laughed. If the tangleleg on her breath hadn't given away her drunkenness, her faltering steps through the foyer would have made the announcement. She had not changed into her working attire and was still wearing black.

"Ma'am, I'd like to see Jesse Cross, please."

"Oh, hell, mister, you don't want none of that when you got all this." She turned, spread her arms wide and fell to the floor.

Brodie jumped to her side and helped her up. He guided her into the parlor where two other women sat in overstuffed chairs that had once been considered fancy. Cloth patches of nearly-matching color ruined the effect. Neither woman moved as Brodie helped the drunken whore to a wicker chair in the corner.

Brodie looked up. "Aren't you two going to help this woman?"

One of the women looked away. The other looked to the stairs leading to the upper floor. "Jesse! It's Olive again."

Olive looked up and sneered. She leaned forward and vomited on the floor.

Brodie heard footsteps coming down the stairs. Jesse Cross stopped halfway down. "My apologies, but sometimes—"

Brodie stood up, wide-eyed. He stepped back.

"Jess Belle Cutler!"

42

Cutler stared at Brodie until a look of recognition registered on her face. She took half a step back. "You!"

Brodie stared, wide-eyed and frozen.

Cutler turned and rushed back upstairs. Her movement broke the spell and Brodie ran across the room.

One of the whores reached out and grabbed his arm. "I got something better for you, Mister. Why don't we—"

He put his hand on her face and shoved her back. She fell onto the chair and landed on the floor. Her curses followed Brodie as he ran up the stairs two at a time. All the doors on the upper floor were closed. He kicked in the first, but the room was empty. He kicked in another. One of the girls was passed out on her bed with a bottle of cheap liquor still in hand. He moved back into the hall, kicked in the door to another empty room and then walked to the last door.

"Don't you come in here!"

Brodie kicked in the door. A short snap of a gunshot followed. The bullet missed and shattered a picture hung on the wall. As Brodie stepped in the room, Cutler twisted the double barrel on her derringer to fire the second bullet. Her hands shook and slowed her actions. When she lifted her head she stared into the barrel of Brodie's .45 Colt. He had already pulled back the hammer.

"Are you sure you want to do that," he said.

Cutler tossed the tiny pistol onto a nearby chair.

"You gonna' kill me, Duphrane?"

"I don't rightly know what I'm going to do."

The corners of her lips just barely moved. It was almost a smile. "Let me fix you a drink."

He gestured toward the bed with his pistol. "Sit down."

She smiled and did as he said. She pulled back the covers.

"None of that."

"On the house, Duphrane."

"All I want from you is answers."

"All I need is questions."

"Why?"

"Men are such idiots." She fluffed a pillow and leaned back.

"For God's sakes, why?"

"You talk too much, Duphrane." She slightly spread her knees. He didn't acknowledge the offer. "Oh, sit down."

Brodie released the hammer on his pistol and eased it into the holster.

Cutler pointed to the chair. "Sit down, Duphrane. This is going to take a while."

Brodie moved over to the chair and picked up the derringer. He dumped the one remaining bullet and sat down.

Cutler leaned over and grabbed a bottle of liquor and a glass from a night stand. She held out the bottle toward Brodie. He shook his head and she poured a drink for herself, emptying the bottle. She swallowed hard and placed the glass back on the stand.

"Like I said, you talk too much. Tule, he heard about you way over here... some kid getting to be real good with a gun planning revenge on the man who killed his ma. Word travels... kid."

"You... how?"

Tule got tired of waiting on you to show up, so we cooked up this idea to flush you out."

"That's how you ended up in Mexican Hat."

"You wasn't all that hard to find, Duphrane."

"We took you in, the whole town. Enid watched over you like a sister."

"That stupid little bitch."

"She's no whore."

"We're all whores, Duphrane. She just trades it for a ring, that's all. Whose ring is she wearing these days? Not yours I bet."

"Shut up."

"I thought you wanted to talk." She smiled and took another drink. "All I had to do was get you started. Once on the move, you'd end up in Tule's territory sooner or later."

"Ambush."

"Sooner or later."

"What happened?"

"Tule got bit by a diamondback. He damn near died out there. When he finally came 'round, he decided it was best to stay dead. Things have been getting kinda' hot for him around here. That, and knowing you were on his trail...."

Brodie stood up. "Where is he?"

"I don't know."

He stepped across the room. Cutler reached down into the drawer on the night stand. Brodie jumped forward, grabbed her by the neck and pulled her off the bed. He let her go, but slapped her hard across her face as she fell back. Blood dripped from her lips. She wiped her mouth. "I was just reaching for another bottle."

Brodie glanced down. The only thing in the drawer was another bottle of liquor. He looked back to Cutler. She dabbed at her mouth with the edge of her sleeve.

Brodie took half a step back and looked at the blood on his right hand. His voice was low and controlled when he spoke. "Where is he?"

"I said I don't know."

Brodie backed up to the door and kicked it shut with his boot. He balled his right hand into a fist.

She laughed softly. It was a sneer. "You and Tule, you ain't all that different, are you?"

Less than fifteen minutes later Brodie came down the stairs and walked through the parlor.

The whore he had pushed sneered. The other said, "Where you goin' in such a hurry, Mister?"

Without pausing or looking back, Brodie said, "Deadman's Ridge."

Part Six

43

As Brodie eased into Lordsburg the sun seared the tops of the ridges to the west. The light scattered, sending alternating rays of gold and gray, like faint wagon spokes, into the darkening sky. He halted in front of the Mint Saloon, but hesitated. He looked up and down the street, at the sunset, and at the sign above the door. Brodie cleared his throat.

"What the hell."

He dismounted and walked quickly from the smell of horse manure and dust into the welcoming odor of whiskey and cigars. Wilhite waved him to the bar.

"Mr. Bock. What'll it be?"

"Just a beer. For now."

Wilhite poured a mug of warm beer. "You find what you been looking for, Mr. Bock?"

"A bit." He sipped his beer. "Is there a halfway decent hotel here?"

"Yes, sir. I'd try Jack Frost over at the café… Frosty's. His name's John, but you know folks. He's usually got a room upstairs – clean and the price ain't bad."

"Thanks." Brodie stared into the golden liquid inside his glass. He tapped his forefinger in a small spot of water on the bar. He looked up to Wilhite. "Do you know of a place called Deadman's Ridge?"

Wilhite wiped the bar before answering. "Can't say so, Mr. Bock. I'll ask around if you want."

"Just curious." He finished his beer, nodded goodbye and walked out the door. He stepped across the street and inside Frosty's Café. The café was crowded with tables and chairs, but only a few were occupied. A portly man carrying a stack of dirty dishes toward the kitchen nodded. "Be right with you." He returned, wiping his hands on a towel. "What'll it be, Mister?"

"Wilhite over at the saloon said you might have a room for the night."

"I do, Mister…."

"Bock. I'll stay the night.

"You look a might hungry. Care to grease your chin before you settle in?"

"I could eat. Yes, Sir."

"Pick yourself a table, Mr. Bock and I'll be right back. It's hash night tonight."

Brodie ate quickly and quietly. He asked about Deadman's Ridge. The owner knew the name, but didn't know how to find it. He offered to ask around. Brodie paid his bill, accepted the room key and was soon asleep.

He woke up to the smell of bacon and coffee from below, cleaned up a bit, and walked downstairs. The small dining room was full of men, mostly miners, wolfing down biscuits, bacon and coffee. They were too focused on cleaning their plates to engage in anything more than minimal conversation.

Brodie settled in at a small table near a window.

Frost arrived with a cup and a pot of coffee. "You'll be wanting a good breakfast before you journey on, Mr. Bock."

Brodie nodded and accepted the coffee. Frost scurried off toward the kitchen. He stopped at a table and spoke to a man finishing off his meal. He nodded back toward Brodie and moved on. The man was young and by the way he was dressed he was probably a ranch hand.

Less than half an hour later Brodie finished his breakfast and settled his bills with Frost. As he stepped out the ranch hand followed.

"Excuse me, Mister."

Brodie turned. "Yes?"

"Wilhite over at the saloon says a man in town is looking for Deadman's Ridge. And you being a stranger, I suspect that'd be you."

"Yeah?"

"I'm headed up that way. If you want to ride along, I'll point you in the right direction when we split the trail."

"What's in it for you, if you don't mind me asking?"

"I like a little conversation on the trail. And all them Apaches they rounded up, well, all of 'em ain't been quite so rounded up, if you know what I mean."

"When are you heading out?"

"Whenever you're ready to go, Mister."

"My horse is down at the stables. I'll meet you back here."

"Done."

They rode north from Lordsburg across a red, dusty plain studded with cactus, scrub and clumps of desert grass. Brodie's guide rambled on about nothing in particular, without asking about Brodie's business or showing any interest in his journey. "They call me Donald Lee and I guess that's as good a name as any. Get this, amigo, back in the States my name really was Smith." He laughed loudly.

Brodie grinned, but his attention was focused on the raw and rugged mountains ahead. He paid no attention to the time until Donald Lee reined in, allowing Brodie to pass by before he, too, stopped.

Donald Lee said, "The trail here heads northeast up Silver City way. Deadman's Ridge is yonder way, just over the Gila." He pointed to a rugged ridgeline to the northwest. A wall of dark gray clouds moved on the other side. Lightning flashes revealed curtains of rain falling up river.

Brodie followed the gesture and looked away.

Donald Lee spoke up. "We'll be headed that way now."

"We?" Brodie turned back. Donald Lee held a .45 caliber Colt pointed at his chest.

"That's right. You and me… Mister Brodie."

44

Brodie reached for his pistol, but the sound of Donald Lee cocking his .45 stopped the motion.

"Smart move. Now hand over the belt."

Brodie unbuckled his gun belt and handed it to his captor. Donald Lee backed away. "You're a smart man, but you talk too much, Brodie."

"Jess Belle."

"She said Tule'd pay good money for you."

Brodie leaned forward. "He's alive."

"Of course, ya' idjit." He gestured to the northeast with his pistol. "You can pick out the trail pretty easy, so get going."

The path was less a trail and more of a series of parallel, low ruts in the deep sand, but the course was easy to follow. They passed a number of low hills, ground down by time into domes of blasted rock. A tall and dark red ridge to their immediate north angled up to a sharp drop off on the western end. The dark wall of storms moved closer and for the first time they could hear thunder after the flash of lightning.

Brodie slowed his pace. "Deadman's Ridge?"

"It might be, if you don't keep moving." His warning was marked by a streak of lightning reaching straight down from cloud to earth. The following thunderclap was deafening.

Brodie moved quickly. They passed the ridge and turned north. Brodie couldn't see the Gila, but he could easily see where it flowed. Ahead was a deep drop off, rugged cliffs sheared from a rocky shelf and a line of green snaking through the desert in a roughly east-west path marked the river. Donald Lee stopped them on the edge of a ridge between two narrow and steep canyons about half a mile apart, each one dropping down to the Gila. Brodie could hear running water. A moment later he could see the glinting sunrays flashing between the greenbelt that marked the river.

"Where's Henderson?"

"Right where you want him, Brodie – Deadman's Ridge."

"Where the hell is that?"

"Get moving."

"Where!"

Donald Lee took a deep breath. He spit and then he pointed across the Gila. Brodie looked over to a grassy plain sloping gently uphill until it reached a wall of shattered rock at the base of a ridge of steep cliffs. "He's on the other side of that. He's waiting on you, ol' Tule is. He's been waiting some time, too. I bet, I just bet he's got something special in mind for you. Now, git on. You can pick out the way."

The trail was little more than an animal run traversing its way down the hill to the cliffs. For much of the ride they looked down on the treetops of tall, green cottonwoods. The sound of rushing water was loud. Brodie saw the churned up, brown waters were dotted with foam. They halted under the cottonwoods and faced a narrow band of swiftly moving water split by a narrow island that was more piled up limbs and tree trunks than sand.

"It's flooding," shouted Brodie.

"Git on across. Tule ain't one for waiting."

"We'll never get through that."

"Move!"

"Look!" Brodie pointed to the east. A large tree recently ripped from the earth floated like a warship on the ocean. As it approached, the leading end submerged and the entire tree was sucked under water. Each man looked down river, but the tree never emerged.

"All right. Back up the hill," Donald Lee said.

"Where to?"

"That point. We'll ride it out there."

Brodie led the way. Donald Lee pointed him to a ledge overlooking the river. The ledge was flat and covered an area about the size of the saloon back in Lordsburg. A narrow crack shaded by the single tree in the area led to a drop off down to the canyon. Another sheer drop off faced the river where the trees below spread out like a carpet. After they dismounted, Donald Lee bound Brodie's wrists behind his back and forced him to sit at the point of the ledge where he was trapped by drop-offs on three sides. Donald Lee tied the horses to the tree. He grabbed a bottle of rye whiskey from his saddle bag and sat down above his prisoner.

Brodie said, "Where's Henderson?"

Donald Lee drank from the bottle. "Damn, that's good."

"Henderson!"

"You're awful anxious to get yourself killed, ain't you?"

"Where is he?"

Donald Lee took another swallow of whiskey and pointed, bottle in hand, across the river and up to the ridge. "On the other side of that – Deadman's Ridge. You'll see him soon enough."

Brodie looked over the ridge. "Where? I don't see him."

"He's got a prospect on the other side. We've been waiting, hell, months to get in there." He drank again. "Damn all Apaches. Well, it's ours now."

Gray clouds moved in from the south, led by small puffs of white that raced ahead. Darker clouds to the west swirled behind Deadman's Ridge and circled back toward the ledge. Large drops of rain occasionally hit the ground. Donald Lee ignored the weather and focused on drinking. Brodie smelled rain on the wind. He squirmed continually to avoid being bitten by the ants that marched across the ledge – large black ants, smaller brown ants and even tiny red ants covered the ground.

Donald Lee, drunk, pulled out his pistol and pointed it at Brodie. "I don' see why I gotta' march your ass 'cross that river an' up that damn hill…." Donald Lee steadied himself with one hand and nearly dropped his bottle. He laughed and took another swallow. "I ought to save Tule the trouble an' jus' shoot you now… or jus' kick you over the cliff." He fired a shot – wide of Brodie but close enough to spray his face with rock fragments. "Nah, Tule, he's gonna' be some surprised when I drag your sad old ass in to camp."

Brodie looked to the ground. All the ants, the thousands that had been scurrying across the ledge were gone. Not a single ant was in sight. He looked up and back to the west. A wall of dark gray moved toward them. Large rain drops hit the ground, a few at a time and then more. Within less than a minute the storm struck with its full force. Powerful winds swirled about and drove the rain in horizontal sheets. Donald Lee's hat flew off his head and was almost instantly lost over the edge and down river. He tried to stand up, but wobbly legs and a powerful gust of wind brought him back to ground. The bottle of rye shattered.

Pea-sized hail fell like a hard shower of rock. Brodie stood up and walked toward the single tree. Donald Lee saw him move and pulled his pistol. He fired and missed, the sound lost in a loud thunderclap. More hail fell – larger this time with stones the size of large plumbs.

"Don't you run on me, Brodie."

"I'm getting under that tree."

"You ain't runnin' on me!" He pulled his pistol and aimed toward Brodie. A hailstone the size of billiard ball struck him in the head and he fell over. The pistol fell from his hand. Brodie rushed toward him, ignoring the pain of the hailstones smashing into his body. Donald Lee struggled to get up. He reached out for the pistol, but Brodie kicked him in the head.

Donald Lee screamed. "I'll kill you!"

Brodie kicked him in the head again and the cracking sound that followed wasn't thunder. Donald Lee shuddered a moment and then was still. Brodie bent over. His captor wasn't breathing. Brodie backed away and ran for the protection of the tree. He crawled under and rode out the storm.

45

Brodie was soaked when the storm finally blew through. He was shaking slightly as the cold seeped into his body. He looked west and north. Another round of storms would soon arrive. He sat down and pulled his bound wrists beneath and then over his legs and feet so that they were in front of his body. The ropes were quickly severed on the edge of a sharp rock. Brodie examined the scene. Both horses had broken free and had run off during the storm. He walked over to Donald Lee and took whatever he could of value – pistol, gun belt, fixed blade knife, a few coins, a box of Lucifers, tobacco and paper. He dragged the man to the edge of the cliff and, without ceremony or pause, kicked him over. The body fell several seconds and then hit the swollen river and was soon sucked under.

Thunderclaps and bolts of lightning announced the arrival of another blast of wind and rain. Still shivering, he walked around the ledge. A crevasse no more than ten feet wide behind the tree revealed a hidden treasure. A wall with a door had been built to enclose a small space within the rock – a man-made space about the size of a closet. The door and wall had been constructed of flat rocks and mud by some ancient benefactor.

Sanctuary!

Brodie scrambled around the ledge and picked up an arm load of small branches from the dry ground beneath the Spruce. He scrambled down the crevasse and tossed them into the small dwelling. He scrambled back up and crawled under the limbs where he scrounged up a large pile of dry needles. He was back inside the enclosure by the time the first raindrops fell. The needles and small twigs were dry enough to spark a few flames and within moments Brodie warmed himself by a small, but comfortable fire. The scent of burning Spruce was like perfume. He leaned back and slowly allowed the shivers to subside.

The storm arrived, a repeat of the earlier event, but the inside of the small dwelling remained dry and out of the wind. Brodie ventured out twice during a few quiet moments within the downpour. He grabbed more small limbs. These were wet, but once split in half or into quarters the dry insides caught and held the fire. He spent a quiet and comfortable night planning how he would find and face Tule Henderson.

46

The clean, cool air of morning at sunrise awakened Brodie. He crawled out of the small dwelling, stretched and climbed up and out of the crevasse. He hugged the north side of the wash behind the scrub brush along the ledge and for some time scanned the ridge across the river. No one appeared to be moving up there and he didn't see anything resembling sunlight glinting off metal or glass.

He must be on the other side like Donald Lee said.

Brodie took stock of his meager possessions and moved quickly across the ledge and into the relative safety of the trees lining the trail down to the Gila. The river had gone down overnight and was near its usual low-water depth. He scrambled down a narrow animal run to the edge where the crossing was shallow and no more than ten or fifteen feet wide. After picking his way through the island of downed trees he crossed a narrow field of rocks that marked the sometimes bottom of the river. He spotted a way up and within minutes was on the sloping hill leading to the ridge. He moved quickly and climbed up through a shallow, rocky wash of gray and pink stone, stopping in a crouch when it played out at the edge of a large field of tall grass, scattered spruce, and soap brush yucca.

The ridge was only a couple of hundred yards away. Its base was a mass of jumbled boulders. Moving around them would be easy, but the rocks led to sheer cliffs several hundred feet high.

No way.

Brodie watched the ridge line, but, again, saw no movement or indication that he was being watched. He moved out of the wash and hurried toward the base of the cliff. He stopped at a soapbrush yucca and plucked a hand full of the white, wafer-like blossoms. He ate them slowly, enjoying equally a taste similar to cucumber and the sensation of something at last in his stomach. He made several more brief stops at yucca plants as he made his way across the open ground.

He was soon against the boulders at the base of the cliffs. He moved west, doing his best to remain unseen from the ridge line. The boulders gradually gave way to a slope on the far western side – a tough scramble, but a reasonable way to reach the ridge line. He started up, traversing a zig-zag line up the hill. The hillside was a mass of loose rock and rubble and he fell several times. With each fall he froze his movements and waited for a bullet to end his struggle. The climb took most of an hour, primarily because he moved slowly and cautiously. When he crested the hill he saw an open field bracketed by the surprisingly narrow rocky edge of Deadman's Ridge and a similar ridge a quarter of a mile to the north.

Between the two ridges was a wide, grassy field leading to a large overhang or cave entrance at the eastern end. He smelled smoke and a whiff of bacon and coffee. A slight movement at the entrance of the overhang caught his attention.

Henderson.

Brodie looked around. The man's camp gave Henderson an unobstructed view of the entire field. The only smart move was to get above that entrance. He'd have to make his way through the rocks above on the south side of the "bowl" that formed a potential killing field for Henderson. A series of pathways, like open trenches, led up to the ridgeline. Brodie used this natural cover to make his way up to a position high above the camp. He watched from the safety of a low-hanging Spruce. Henderson was no longer in sight, so Brodie waited. Hours passed with no movement coming from the camp.

He must be inside that cave. Now? Or do I wait?

Now.

Brodie stepped out and moved on, picking his way among the rocks and boulders. As he moved closer he could hear the faint sounds of metal striking rock. He could see the camp better. The cave was really a large overhang, a natural shelter going back 20 or 30 feet into the rock. A horse, staked to a long rope, grazed on the tall grass nearby. Henderson was alone.

Brodie eased the pistol from its holster and moved forward. He came to a break in the rocks. Instead of making his way around the drop off, he jumped. His right foot landed on the edge of the break. A slab of rock gave way and he fell. He landed hard and with two consequences. One, his head slammed into an out crop and he was knocked unconscious. Two, when his body hit the hard surface, the fall caused him to pull the trigger on his pistol. The weapon fired.

And the sound of metal against stone inside the enclosure stopped.

47

Brodie awoke to the smell of boiling coffee and the painful sensations of pain in his ankle and his head. He kept his eyes closed and listened.

Henderson spoke. "No use pretending, Mister. I heard you sniffing."

Brodie opened his eyes and looked around. He was inside the opening with the overhang, which was a far larger space than it had looked from a distance. A man-made cave led to darkness at the far back wall. The open space had been made livable with rough-hewn furniture crafted from the nearby trees. Henderson poured a cup of coffee and approached. He offered it to Brodie.

It was only then that Brodie discovered his hands were tied at the wrists. He accepted the cup.

Henderson stepped back. "I thought I'd find out what the hell you're up to before I kill you."

Brodie nodded and sipped the coffee. His head throbbed, but the drink helped. "Thanks."

"Who the hell are you and what are you doing up here?"

Brodie stared at his captor. The monster of his imagination was in reality a plain and dirty little man, the kind someone passes in the street without noticing. His face was impassive, but his eyes were dark and probing. Brodie said, "My name's the same as yours... Smith."

Henderson laughed. "Ah... I hate killing a man with a sense of humor."

"Then don't." Brodie finished the coffee and offered the tin cup back to its owner.

"More?"

"Thanks."

Henderson poured a second cup and brought it back. "I been Mr. Smith a few times in my life, too. Now, why the hell are you up here?"

"You need a new partner."

"What the hell's that supposed to mean?"

"Donald Lee sent me… with a message. You're Henderson, Tule Henderson, right?"

"Yeah."

"You want to untie me now?"

"Not just yet."

"That man you're hunting, the man that's hunting you, he's sniffing around Lordsburg."

"Hell, I know that."

"Donald Lee thinks somebody told him about this place?"

"Why ain't Donald Lee tellin' me this himself?"

"Because he got drunk…."

"That's him all right."

"And shot himself in the foot. He might lose it."

"How do you figure in all this?"

"I was getting drunk with him at the time. He pulled his pistol. I guess he was going to plug the ceiling. He plugged himself instead. Stupid son of a bitch. Long story short, he said you needed to know something fast and that you'd make it worth my while." Brodie held up his wrists.

Henderson looked at him for a considerable time and then cut the bindings. "I got me a partner."

"A one legged drunk don't make for much of a team, Henderson."

"Call me Tule." He kicked at the dirt with the heel of his boot. "And you're right. Stick around at least until you heal up. Then we'll see."

"Sounds fair."

And then we'll see.

48

Brodie's head wound was bloody, but minor and the cuts and scrapes healed quickly. His ankle wasn't broken, but it was severely sprained and he was unable to walk more than a few yards at a time. Henderson proved to be a genial, if mistrustful host. He cared for Brodie's needs, but kept his weapons put up in a niche carved out of the rock and he always positioned himself between the weapons and his guest. Brodie worked to put the man at ease as best he could.

Henderson stepped out to urinate and when he returned Brodie stood at the edge of the mine shaft. Henderson said, "Stay out of there."

"This ain't much of a working mine."

"That there is my… meat locker. It ain't none of your business."

Brodie sat down on a bench next to the opening.

Henderson sat down on another. "You any good with a gun?"

"I hit what I aim at."

"Ever kill a man?"

Brodie looked down and then up. He smiled. "That's why my name is Smith."

Henderson laughed. It was genuine and infectious. Brodie joined in. Henderson stood up and looked out the enclosure. "Do you think you can shoot us a rabbit for supper?"

"How many do you want?"

"Take my horse and ride over to the drop off. There's plenty of 'em out that way."

Brodie stood up and walked to Henderson's saddle. His limp was barely noticeable.

Henderson's pleasant expression turned sour. "Don't you come back for an hour or so."

"Whatever you say."

He handed Brodie a rifle. "If you don't see me, shout out before you come in."

"Yeah."

Henderson kept his hand on his sidearm as Brodie left.

Brodie saddled the horse and rode west. He glanced back in time to see Henderson enter the mine shaft.

The tall grasses were teaming with rabbits, but Brodie waited. When he reached the western end of the small plain he extended his arm, palm open and held sideways to gauge the time. The sun rested on his little finger and the distant horizon was just beneath his thumb. *An hour until sundown.*

He waited almost the full hour before shooting two rabbits – each a clean head shot. He skinned and gutted each and then rode directly back to the overhang, shouting out when he approached. Henderson stood up and waved him in. He had a fire going and a spit in place. Brodie offered him the rifle. Henderson shook his head. "Put it up yourself. If you was going to kill me you'd have made your move already. You'd be dead for trying, 'course."

Brodie placed the rifle in a hand-hewn rack placed on the floor. He soon had the rabbits on the spit and the smell of roasting meat filled the enclosure. After eating, Brodie said, "It's obvious you ain't mining in here. Do you think you can tell your new partner what the hell you *are* doing out here?"

Henderson pulled off a last bite of meat from a rabbit leg. He tossed the bone into the fire, chewed a minute and then spoke. "There's gold out here, and silver, but it ain't in the mining kind."

"Stagecoach?"

"Have you got something against that line of work?"

"I'm against shotgun riders."

"Well, partner, I got good news for you. The kind of gold and silver I'm talking about has already been robbed."

"If you done robbed them coaches, what do you need me for?"

"With the Apaches gone, white folks will be moving into this country. I need somebody to watch my back. Besides, all the robbing's been done."

Brodie stared into the fire. He stirred the coals with a stick. "Apaches?"

"Yes, sir! They been robbing stages, freight wagons, pilgrims, hell, even the army, for years. Lots of years. And I've been waiting years for somebody to kill or run off them bastards. Thank you, U.S. Army."

"And you figure it's hid up in these hills?"

"It's got to be. The Apaches hit down Lordsburg way… Deming, Steins, Tableau, all them towns are down there. The Apaches live in the mountains up north. This here country between is littered with mines and prospects."

"Perfect hiding places."

"Especially, if you got the run of the land. Well, they ain't got the run of the land no longer. And that gold and silver is mine. Ours. All we got to do is find it."

"There's a lot of ground to cover up here."

Henderson stood up. He walked over to the small wood pile and returned with a handful of sticks. He built up the fire. "We'll cross the river tomorrow. There's a ranch down toward Tableau. We'll get you a horse and outfit there."

"I ain't carrying much money."

"You won't need it."

"Oh."

"Tomorrow."

Brodie walked across the room, picked up Henderson's saddle and stepped outside.

Tomorrow then.

49

Brodie, asleep, rolled over. The movement startled two crows pecking around the entrance to Henderson's hide out. The flapping and caw-cawing woke him up. The field in front of the camp was just turning an early morning shade of gold. He sat up and looked around. Henderson's bedroll was empty. He stood up and glanced to the niche carved into the wall. His pistol and gun belt were in place. A cough from deep inside the mine shaft stopped him from moving on. The light of a kerosene lamp indicated Henderson's immediate arrival.

Henderson stepped out and stretched. "Killing stirs up my blood."

"Killing?"

"You don't think that rancher's going to just give us your horse, do you?"

"Is killing necessary?"

"For some folks."

Brodie gathered up several small sticks from a pile of wood in the corner and started building the base of a fire.

Henderson offered the lantern. "I'll make the coffee. Take this."

Brodie stood up and took the lantern.

Henderson grinned. "There's something back in the mine that'll warm you up better 'n coffee." He squatted down and began to finish Brodie's work. "Go on. I'll have the coffee ready when you're through."

"Through with what?"

Henderson's grin grew bigger. "Go on."

Brodie walked to the open shaft and stepped inside. He looked over his shoulder. Henderson hadn't put on his gun belt. He was still squatting by the pile of sticks. His low growl of a laugh ushered Brodie further into the mine shaft.

The passage was deep and the soft bubble of light from the lantern barely lit the darkness. He moved slowly, stepping over the occasional rotted plank and keeping an eye out for drop offs. The shaft turned left and within a few steps the entrance was out of sight. Brodie stopped and cocked his head.

What the hell?

He heard sobbing, muffled sobs. The voice was high pitched. He moved forward. The light revealed the end of the tunnel and a pile of blankets. Someone was beneath them.

"What the hell?"

"Please... no...."

Brodie stepped closer and tugged back one of the blankets. A young woman, a girl in her early teens by the looks of her, curled up in a fetal position. "Don't... no more today...."

Brodie pulled the blanket back up so that she was fully covered. "You're just a kid."

"Please...."

Brodie rocked back half a step. "I'm not going to hurt you, girl. I promise."

"Just don't cut me no more."

"I'm not going to even touch you."

Her eyes were wide with fear. "I'll be nice. Just don't cut on me again."

He held the lamp up to his face. "Look. I'm not Henderson."

"You're that Donald man."

"Girl, listen."

Her face was blank as if she had sent her mind to some other place.

"I'm going to get you out of this. I promise."

She looked to the roof, her eyes glassy, and slowly pulled away the blanket. Brodie grabbed it and pulled it back up to her neck.

"That's never going to happen to you again. I promise.

"I'll be nice." Her voice was soft and distant. "I'll be nice...."

Brodie stood up and walked away, taking the lantern with him. His breathing was steady and deep. As he approached the entrance he slowed down and stopped.

No weapon.

Henderson squatted by the fire with his back to the mine entrance. He wore his gun belt. Brodie stepped back and took a deep breath.

One chance.

He unscrewed the cap on the lantern and turned up the flame. Without hesitating he stepped out and threw the lantern. It struck Henderson in the back, spilling oil and then flame. Henderson turned and reached for his pistol as he stood. Brodie screamed as he ran to Henderson and shoved him into the fire. The flame on Henderson's jacket spread. He rolled over in the rocky dirt several times to dampen the flames, losing his pistol in the process. Brodie grabbed the coffee pot from the ground and flung it at Henderson. It struck him in the face. He rolled again and came up with a Bowie knife in his hand.

Henderson charged, his jacket leaving a trail of smoke through the enclosure. Brodie side-stepped and kicked out, tripping his opponent. Henderson lost his balance and fell. The knife slid across the floor. Brodie rushed to the niche in the wall and grabbed his pistol. Henderson was up on all fours, but he stopped moving when he saw the .45 aimed at his heart. His breathing was heavy. "What the hell?"

"Don't move. I don't want to kill you just yet."

"Wha—"

"Do you remember Mexican Hat?"

"What Mexican?"

"Utah! You and your brother?"

Henderson got up on his knees. He stared at Brodie. "You're him."

"Brodie."

"I thought I had you killed."

Brodie cocked the hammer on his .45.

Henderson sat back with his butt on his heels. "Yeah. I remember. I cut on your momma some." He grinned. "I think she liked having a real ma—"

Brodie fired. When Henderson fell over, Brodie fired again. Three more bullets ripped into the man's body before he stopped shooting. He stood still for several moments before walking over and squatting down. "Was it worth it?"

He sat down and continued looking at the body of the man he had hated, hunted. Moments passed. Brodie looked from the body to the blood on his hands and back to the body.

Later, when he brought out the girl, he made her look at Henderson's body.

"See, girl. That's what happens to men like him."

She stared for a moment and then looked to Brodie. Her eyes were full of fear and confusion.

"Nobody is going to hurt you ever again."

The corners of her lips barely curled up and into a slight smile. She hugged Brodie. She still held him close as they rode off to the west.

Behind them, the vultures circled above Henderson's camp. Brodie glanced back one last time as they approached the western edge of the field.

Was it... was it worth it?

His head barely moved – a nod.

"Enid." His voice was a lonely sigh. And a prayer.

50

Several people in Lordsburg recognized the girl. She and her older brother had disappeared several weeks earlier while riding back from church. The boy's body and their wagon was found in a dry wash east of town. There was no sign of the girl. The incident was one of those crimes in which everyone knows who did it, but no one could prove it or do anything about it. He took her to the restaurant where a small group of women soon gathered. A rider galloped off to her family's ranch to bring her parents the good news. Brodie said only that he had found her north of town. While the attention was focused on the girl, he slipped out, mounted his horse and rode away.

Brodie's long journey back to Mexican Hat followed the same route that had taken him away. He pushed on from before sunrise until well after sunset every day. He avoided towns and settlements except for necessary stops to purchase supplies. When meeting someone on the trail he nodded an acknowledgement, but never spoke. Each night he dozed off mentally building the ranch home and the ranch life he and Enid could now share. Each morning the burden of loneliness became lighter as he moved closer to home.

After many hard, but uneventful weeks on the trails and roads he at last rested on the hills overlooking Mexican Hat. He looked over the town and let his eyes rest on Enid's home. He took in a long breath of air blowing up from the San Juan. His face curled into an unpleasant expression.

"Damn." *I can't let her see me like this. Or smell me.*

He moved on and headed out to his ranch.

The elongated pile of earth under a cottonwood behind the ranch sent a cold feeling down his spine. The rectangle was lined with river rocks and topped off with a cross of wood painted white. He rode up and read the name.

Juan Galleta
A Good Hand
A Better Friend

"Oh, Damn."

Brodie dismounted and stared at his friend's grave for a long time before walking his horse over to the ranch. He removed the saddle and took the animal to the corral. Brodie entered the house.

"Dukie!" He shouted knowing no one would respond.

Brodie pulled down a large wash tub from a peg on the wall and filled it with water from the kitchen pump. He bathed, shaved and was making a pot of coffee when he heard shouting from outside.

"Brodie!"

Dukie burst into the house, rushed across the room and grabbed Brodie by the arms. "There is a God."

Brodie hugged his friend. "There must be, Dukie. There must be."

An awkward moment of silence passed as each man avoided the obvious. Brodie poured two cups of coffee. "Juan?"

"Renegades. Navajos we think. They got him down river. I was in town buying a mule."

"I should have been here."

"Don't think like that, Brodie. If you was here it could have been you. Or me. It doesn't pay to think like that."

"I still—"

"Still, hell. You're back. That's all that counts. You're back."

Another silence passed. Dukie finally spoke. "Did you get him?"

"Yeah."

"Alive... or?"

"Or."

Dukie nodded. He brightened up. "Well, youngster, you're back. It's time to start some living again."

"I can't wait to see the look on Enid's face."

Dukie frowned. "You haven't been into town yet?"

"I thought I'd better clean up first. Hell, if the sight of me didn't scare her the smell sure.... What's wrong?"

"Sit down, Brodie."

Brodie didn't go into Mexican Hat until the following morning. He rode down the main street past the McCutchen place and to the edge of town. He stopped and dismounted at a newly constructed home. He walked to the front door and knocked. Within a moment Enid opened the door.

Brodie removed his hat. "Mrs. Adelson."

Enid stepped back, her eyes wide with shock. "Brodie."

"Yes, Ma'am. I've come to pay my respects."

Enid stepped out onto the porch and shut the door. She looked him over. "You have lost weight."

"I've lost more than that it seems."

Enid dropped her head and then looked back up. "You left me, Brodie."

"I was always coming back. You knew that."

"How could I?" Her voice betrayed a touch of anger.

"Enid, I...."

"Father's getting old, Brodie. There aren't many fit men in Mexican Hat. A woman...."

Brodie stepped back and put on his hat. "I just came by to wish you well, Enid. I'll be going now."

"What was I supposed to do, Brodie?"

He looked at her with disbelief and then put on his hat. "Mrs. Adelson." He nodded, mounted his horse and rode back to the ranch.

Later that day Dukie led his younger partner on a sundown tour of the ranch. "I can't stay," Brodie said.

"I figured from the look on your face when you got back from town."

"Enid was always part of this. Now...."

Dukie remained silent for a moment. "I... we got an offer for the ranch a while back. A man from Arizona has made an offer, a good one."

"Take it."

"Are you sure?"

"I have to move on."

"Yeah, that bug has bitten me, too. Ever since Juan got shot, it hasn't been the same."

"Where are you heading?"

"I've been thinking about Mexico. Juan's folks are down there. If they're half as good as him, I just might fit myself in. How about you?"

"I don't know. I've been living on revenge so long... a man needs a reason to live, Dukie. And now with Enid married off, I just feel a whole lot of empty."

"Juan always said a man needs a reason to live beyond just living. Forget Enid and find yourself some other woman, a good woman, to take care of."

They rode on, stopping at a bluff overlooking the river. Brodie said, "I'm going to stay out here tonight. Do some thinking."

"I'll have the coffee on when you come in. You are coming back in, aren't you?"

"Yeah. I just need to start looking for that reason to live, something to fill up that empty place."

Dukie rode off. Brodie gathered some wood and soon had a fire going. He stared into the flames until the fire died down to red embers on a dark ground. As the gray light of a false dawn turned to pale gold and then bright yellow, Brodie stood up.

"I know."

51

Thomas J. Ferris glanced at his watch and reached for the telephone on his desk. He put the receiver to his ear and clicked the handle several times. "Maylene, connect me... Tom Ferris, you know my voice... Okay, connect me with the missus." A moment later he spoke again. "It's me. I forgot to tell you, I'll be late coming home. Yes, Ma'am, but I have to run out to Bock's Canyon. No, everything is all right. I just need to make a delivery. Okay. By, hon."

He clicked the handle again. "Maylene, get me... dagnabbit, it's Tom Ferris again. Get me Brodie's place." A few seconds later he said, "Maria, Tom Ferris. Is Brodie there? All right, just tell him that medicine he ordered is in. I'm bringing it out now, that and a few things I know you all will be needing. I'll be there in about an hour. Tell him, now. Bye."

He placed the phone back on his desk and stepped out of his office and into the retail space of Ferris Mercantile. He spoke to his assistant. "Have you loaded up the contraption?"

"Yes, sir."

"Take care of things for a while. I'm going out to Bock's Canyon."

"Tell 'em hello for me."

Ferris stepped outside and walked to his Model T, where he cranked the handle. The engine sputtered a couple of times and then started. He jumped in and drove west out of Apache Junction and onto the road between Mesa and Globe. The dirt road was dusty and rutted, but had been used so long and by so many vehicles that it was rock hard in dry weather. The Superstition Mountains towered over the skyline to the north as he puttered along. He pulled off to the side of the road when he reached a rutted, rocky road leading into the south side of the mountain range. A sign pegged to a four-by-four post in the ground read *Bock's Canyon*.

He had to wait only a few minutes until the rattling of a wagon bouncing down the twisting road and the cloud of dust that followed indicated the approach of his customer. He and Brodie waved at each other at the same time. Ferris grabbed a wooden box from the automobile.

Brodie reined in his horse and pulled the wagon next to the automobile. "Maria said you were headed our way."

"That medicine you wanted came in. How is the missus?"

Brodie took off his hat, wiped his brow and ran his fingers through his graying hair. "Good days and bad, Tom, good days and bad."

"Well, maybe this'll help some."

"Maybe."

"I got a few other things in there I thought you'd be wanting. It's all on account."

Brodie looked through the box. "Thanks, Tom. I'll settle up at the end of the month as usual."

Ferris climbed aboard the Model T. "You all ought to come in to town some time. We got what they call a comedy review, one of those traveling shows, coming in this weekend. Do you good."

"Thanks, but I don't think she's—"

"Hell, Brodie, folks in town think you hung the moon. No one's going to say anything."

"I'll think about it."

"Don't think, Brodie. Just do."

"We'll see."

Brodie cranked the Model T to life and held his horse steady as Ferris drove off. He stepped up into the wagon and started up the road into Bock's Canyon. The road led to a comfortable ranch shaded by tall cottonwoods nourished by a spring-fed creek. He pulled the wagon into the barn, released the horse into the corral, and carried the small box toward the house. A short, slim woman, an Apache, stepped out of the door. He handed over the box.

"Here you go, Maria. You know where to put everything."

"The medicine?"

"It's in there. I saw where Tom stuffed in another catalog, too. So, I guess I know what you and the missus will be doing all week."

"She is having a good day, Brodie."

"I think we're having more this year than ever."

"I think you are right" Maria opened the door and paused. "I will have supper in an hour or so. Why don't you watch the sundown? The two of you."

Brodie followed her in. A moment later he pushed a wheelchair through the door and positioned it so the woman was shaded by the porch, yet had the best view of the landscape dropping off to the south. He sat down in a chair beside her and took her hand. She turned her head his way and the corners of her lips formed a smile.

Brodie beamed. "This *is* a good day, Grace. It truly is." He wasn't quite sure, but the slight pressure from her hand on his seemed real.

END

Also by Dan Baldwin

The Practical Pendulum

Find Me (As Told to Dan Baldwin)

Just the Facts, Please, About Alcohol and Drug Abuse
(With George Sewell)

Streetwise Landlording and Property Management
(With Mark B. Weiss)

Streetwise Restaurant Management
(With John R. James)

Caldera

Caldera II – A Man on Fire

Caldera III – A Man of Blood

Desecration – An Ashley Hayes Mystery

Heresy – An Ashley Hayes Mystery

Vengeance – An Ashely Hayes Mystery

Trapp Canyon

Bock's Canyon

Sparky and the King

Vampire Bimbos on Spring Break (Short Story Collection)

All Dan Baldwin books are available in e-book and paperback formats from Amazon, CreateSpace, Smashwords, B&N, and other major distributors.

Contact Dan Baldwin at baldco@msn.com or visit his websites www.fourknightspress.com and www.danbaldwin.biz

About the Author

Dan Baldwin is the author, co-author or ghostwriter of more than 50 books on business. He is the author of the Caldera series of westerns, Trapp Canyon, a western, the Ashley Hayes mysteries Desecration, Heresy and Vengeance, and the thriller Sparky and the King. He is the winner of numerous local, regional, and national awards for writing and directing film and video projects. He earned an Honorable Mention from the Society of Southwestern Authors writing competition for his short story Flat Busted and earned a Finalist designation from the National Indie Excellence Awards for Trapp Canyon. Baldwin is a resident of Phoenix-Mesa and travels extensively throughout Caldera's West.

A Four Knights Press Publication
www.fourknightspress.com

Made in the USA
Charleston, SC
10 January 2016